She'd given up everything for her country

A family and a husband, not to mention children, were not in her future and they never would be. She'd traded those things for adrenaline and power, and it was way too late to go back and make changes.

If she'd ever had a chance at having any of those things, it would have been with Haden. He'd been wild, but under the craziness there had been a rock-solid man she'd come to care for more than she'd expected. More than anyone she'd ever cared for before–or since. He'd been special and rare–one of those guys who caught you unaware when you'd decided no one else could possibly surprise you.

For a single second she wanted to walk away and ignore the decision she'd wrestled with for the past five hours, but she knew that wasn't a real option.

If she didn't take the job, then someone else would.

Haden was a dead man walking.

Dear Reader,

In philosophical circles around the world, debates have raged since Aristotle's times over the "greater good" versus the rule of self-interest. What is best for society as a whole can sometimes differ from what is best for an individual. In other words, if the city wants to put a new highway through your backyard, the commuters will be thrilled, but you might not be quite as happy.

Extrapolate this argument into a life-and-death situation and you have the basis for THE OPERATIVES series and especially for *Not Without Cause*. The question I wanted to examine was this one: If a war could be ended by killing one individual—and thereby saving the lives of thousands—what should be done? Just to complicate matters, since I write love stories, I added another issue to the mix, as well. What if the someone who had to be killed was someone you loved?

Not Without Cause is the story of how two people come together, despite their opposition, and work to achieve what is best. In the process, their love grows even stronger and they realize how deep their feelings for each other—and for their country—really run. When the choices are this tough, nothing is easy.

I wanted the final story in THE OPERATIVES series to be a special one. I needed to write something that was entertaining but at the same time presented some questions that would make everyone think a bit. Our world is changing daily—hourly, in fact—and some very hard choices are being made. The sacrifices those decisions entail aren't easy ones because they touch the rights and truths we all hold dear.

Meredith and Haden understand that emotions come with a price, and their willingness to pay that price is a testament to the power of love, be it their love for each other, their love for freedom, or their love for their country. Sharing their story with my readers is my way for sharing that love, as well. I hope you enjoy *Not Without Cause*.

Kay David

NOT WITHOUT CAUSE
Kay David

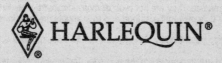

HARLEQUIN®

TORONTO • NEW YORK • LONDON
AMSTERDAM • PARIS • SYDNEY • HAMBURG
STOCKHOLM • ATHENS • TOKYO • MILAN • MADRID
PRAGUE • WARSAW • BUDAPEST • AUCKLAND

ISBN 0-373-71338-X

NOT WITHOUT CAUSE

Copyright © 2006 by Carla Luan.

www.eHarlequin.com

Printed in U.S.A.

Books by Kay David

HARLEQUIN SUPERROMANCE
798–THE ENDS OF THE EARTH
823–ARE YOU MY MOMMY?
848–THE MAN FROM HIGH MOUNTAIN
888–TWO SISTERS
945–OBSESSION
960–THE NEGOTIATOR*
972–THE COMMANDER*
985–THE LISTENER
1045–MARRIAGE TO A STRANGER
1074–DISAPPEAR
1131–THE TARGET*
1149–THE SEARCHERS
1200–SILENT WITNESS
1230–THE PARTNER
1303–NOT WITHOUT HER SON**
1321–NOT WITHOUT THE TRUTH**

SIGNATURE SELECT SAGA
NOT WITHOUT PROOF**

*The Guardians
**The Operatives

Don't miss any of our special offers. Write to us at the
following address for information on our newest releases.

Harlequin Reader Service
U.S.: 3010 Walden Ave., P.O. Box 1325, Buffalo, NY 14269
Canadian: P.O. Box 609, Fort Erie, Ont. L2A 5X3

This book is dedicated to the men and women
who have served in the United States military forces,
present, past and future.

Thank you for your courage,
your sacrifice and your dedication.

PROLOGUE

Guatemala City, Guatemala
May 2006

JACK HADEN HAD the taxi driver drop him three blocks from his rented villa. Walking down the dimly lit sidewalk, scanning the gloom, his weapon handy, he found himself wondering how it would feel to have a regular job with two kids and a dog and a wife all waiting for him in a nice little home on a nice wide street.

What would it be like not to worry about someone following you and shooting you in the back? Haden had a hunch he'd never know, but more and more lately, the question had been on his mind.

The idea plagued him for a second longer, then he wondered why he was even wondering. He was forty years old and he'd lived on the edge since the day he'd left his mother's home. If things ever did change, he'd probably end up restless, screw the nanny and start drinking like a fish.

Either way, he wasn't going to have a chance to find out so why was he even thinking about it?

He turned down the street one block south of his house. Shadows clung to the houses and lay across the walls like woven *chamarras*. Guatemala City was always dark, even when the street lamps were on. Back in the nineties when the political situation had been even crazier than it was now, the powers that be had kept it that way for a reason, and although things had changed—slightly—the place was still blacker than hell, literally and metaphorically speaking.

Even in Zona 10.

Divided into sectors for ease of reference, Guatemala City had a personality of its own and each area had a unique flavor as well. Zona 10, where he'd had dinner, was upscale all the way and it housed the offices and shops the foreigners frequented. The restaurants were typically more expensive, the streets were generally cleaner and the neighborhoods were usually safer. A lot of the diplomats lived in Zona 10. He'd attended a party there last week at the French ambassador's home. Haden wasn't quite sure why he'd been included—except his name had gotten on a list when he'd first moved to Guatemala City and the list had been passed around. For years he'd had somewhere to go every night if he wanted. No one knew what, or who, he actually was and most of the time he passed on the invitations, but that night he'd been ready for some company, his mood overtaking his usual reluctance to mingle with expats who had little to do and even less to say.

Still, the guy from Washington had taken him by surprise.

"So you work at the American Embassy, huh?" he'd asked, the bourbon in his hand obviously not his first. Their hostess had introduced the man to Haden as Brad Prescott, a communications engineer in town for work. "What are you, a spy or something?"

Haden had had a smart-aleck answer ready but at the last minute, he'd stuck with his normal cover story. "I wish! Nah, my job's not that glamorous. I'm just a computer technician."

Prescott had nodded, then stirred his drink with his finger and licked it with a sloppy motion. "Too bad," he'd mumbled. "I thought you might know someone I know back in Washington." He'd leaned closer, a whiff of cigarette smoke coming with him as his voice dropped in a self-important way. "He's with the Agency and he's a ruthless SOB. We're partners in a little start-up venture I'm handling."

Haden had pursued the conversation because he'd had nothing better to do. "Who is he? You never know, he could be my old neighbor or something."

The tall blonde laughed in a condescending manner. "I doubt that. This guy doesn't have neighbors or friends. He's too rich for either, but I don't think he'll have that little problem much longer. I'm gonna help him out in that department."

"Well, what's his name anyway? Maybe I've worked on his computer," Haden joked.

Prescott shook his head again. "Dean Reynolds with a computer? He doesn't need a computer, he's half machine himself!" Prescott had muttered something else then stumbled off, Haden watching until the man had been absorbed into the crowd.

He'd been with the CIA too long because Haden immediately assumed he was being set up. He'd studied Prescott for another hour, then followed the man when the party was over. Prescott had gone directly to the Marriott and as far as Haden could tell, had stayed there the rest of the night. The next day, Haden had paid his way past security and searched the engineer's hotel room but found nothing.

Two days later, Prescott disappeared.

He was snatched right off the road in broad daylight. No one seemed to know where he was but rumor had it Rodrigue Vega's men had been involved. When Haden had picked up that bit of gossip, his radar had pinged even louder.

For months, he'd been hearing snatches of information linking someone in Washington with a unique smuggling operation based in Guatemala

City. If the rumors were correct, Haden didn't even want to think about the possibilities. Taking dope and illegals over the border was one thing; slipping in terror and its providers was something else. One of the names out of Washington that had been mentioned as being behind the deal—Dean Reynolds—had surprised Haden. But not totally.

He didn't trust Dean Reynolds. Not after that deal in Libya. If Reynolds, the director of the CIA, *had* somehow managed to hook up with one of the biggest crooks in Guatemala City, Rodrigue Vega, they would have a huge network of assets—of people and of funds—at their disposal. The results could be catastrophic, because neither man gave a damn about anything. Reynolds had hidden behind a screen of patriotic fervor for years, his power and influence growing to match his ego. Vega, once a petty thief, now part drug lord, part pseudo-politician, held tremendous power in Guate, especially within the vast communities of immigrants who made the city their home. Both men were greedy, egotistical and self-centered bastards the world would have been better off without. In Haden's humble opinion.

Haden worked the pieces of the puzzle as he walked, but as usual, more questions than answers resulted from his effort.

Two minutes later, he turned the corner to the street where he lived. A movement in the darkness caught his eye and he checked his progress, his hand going to his waistband without conscious thought. When two hissing cats streaked by, he exhaled slowly, his fingers falling back to his side.

Had his meeting with Prescott been a coincidence? Had the engineer really been kidnapped or was he already dead? Had Prescott's alcohol-soaked brain been behind the mention of his association with Reynolds or had the revelation been guided by something more sinister?

Haden approached the patch of light that revealed the gate to his courtyard. Pulling his key from his pocket, he unfastened the bolt set in the iron bars and stepped inside. Light from a lamp in his neighbor's house fell through a tree in the courtyard and cast shadows on him as he continued forward. The sounds of a television down the street rippled through the cool night air. Deep in thought, he unlocked his front door, walked inside and closed the door behind him.

The first blow hit him across the shoulders.

The second one sent him to the floor.

The third strike filled his mouth with the salty taste of blood. He spit it out, then his vision went black.

CHAPTER ONE

A Starbucks by the Galleria
Houston, Texas
Late May 2006

"YOU'RE THE ONLY PERSON who can do this, Meredith. There's no one else I trust." Dean Reynolds tapped his paper coffee cup against the table and then looked up. "There's no one else I'd even ask."

Meredith Santera stared at the man sitting on the other side of the small, black table. Six years had passed since the last time she'd seen him and that meeting had been under decidedly different circumstances. They'd been in Dean's office, with its perfect view of the Memorial Garden and the haze of D.C. in the distance. He'd had on a black suit, she remembered, and a red tie, his shirt so white it had dazzled her almost as much as the voice coming out of his speakerphone.

"Yes, Mr. President, she's here right now." Reynolds had winked at her, then waved his hand toward the phone. The seriousness of the situation over-coming her, Meredith had stuttered and stumbled and made a fool of herself, but the president had been gracious.

She sipped her coffee then put down the cup. "I was shocked when you called. I never expected to hear directly from you. We agreed—"

Dean leaned infinitesimally closer, his back ram-rod straight. "I know what we agreed, but I couldn't trust anything except a face-to-face on this one." He seemed to force himself to relax and gave her what passed for his smile. "I hope it wasn't too much of an inconvenience for you to meet me."

"Seeing you could never be anything but a plea-sure, Dean. You should know that by now."

Meredith patted the older man's hand. He was the same age her father would have been were he still alive and the two men had always reminded her of each other with their similar military backgrounds, their staunch patriotism and their love of all things convoluted.

But she hadn't wanted to meet with Reynolds when he'd called and obviously he'd sensed that during their short conversation. He'd said just enough to make her want to hear more but trepida-tion had come with it. Her father had passed away six months ago from a stroke and she missed him like crazy. They'd been business partners as well as parent and child, their relationship particularly close since Meredith's mom had died while Meredith had been in college, a brain tumor taking her within months of its discovery. Since her father's death, Meredith had questioned every decision she'd made.

Just as she was doing now.

She toyed with her napkin, folding the edges, then smoothing them, the metal grids on the table making a pattern from below. "I'm just not sure I can help you with this…situation," she said reluctantly. "You may be talking to the wrong person."

"I disagree and so does the man I report to. He wants you in on this and you and I both know why." He paused. "It's important, Meredith, or I wouldn't even be asking you."

"He" was the president but neither of them acknowledged that fact.

"I understand what you're saying, Dean, but one of our own?" She shook her head at the enormity of what he was asking.

"I know…I know. It doesn't feel right, does it?"

He sounded sad as he asked the question that needed no answer. "All I can say is that we have no other option. We have to stop these people. Think about 9/11. You would have done anything to prevent that disaster, just like I would have."

"Are you talking about something that big?"

"Yes. Potentially worse. These aren't migrant

farm workers Jack Haden is smuggling from Mexico, Meredith. They're terrorists from Syria. Every one of them is a member of Al Balsair."

Meredith drew a deep breath at the name of the violent group. "That just doesn't sound like the Haden I knew. Dammit, Dean, he's the last guy I'd expect to get involved in something like this."

Reynolds's mouth tightened at her curse, just as her father's would have. "My information is as reliable as information gets. Jack Haden's turned and you have to take care of him. If you don't, he's going to help some of the worst terrorists alive get a free pass into the United States. I don't want that happening on my watch, Meredith, and you shouldn't, either. He's a traitor."

She gripped her cup and wished she had a flask of something—anything—that she could add to what was left of her coffee.

Jack Haden had been her boss at the Agency, but he'd been better in bed than behind the desk. Short and violent as a spring storm, their top-secret relationship had been chaotic and disastrous. Then Dean had called her into his office for that historic meeting and the Operatives, her team of specialists, had been born.

The night she'd informed Haden she was leaving the Agency, they'd had two hours of incredible sex, then afterward, when she'd revealed as much as she could about her plans, he'd thrown her out of his apartment. She'd been so unprepared for his reaction she'd ended up on his front porch clutching more of her clothing to her chest than she'd actually been able to get on her body.

She'd told herself the breakup had been bound to happen. Sooner or later, she and Haden would have killed one another. One would have shot the other or they would have screwed themselves to death. Sometimes, though, she wondered where the relationship might have gone. Haden had been an intriguing man with secrets that didn't match the person she'd come to care for and the contrast had kept her interested far longer than normal. She would have figured him out eventually—but it might have taken her a lifetime.

"I brought Jack Haden into the Agency so believe me, this wasn't an easy decision." Reynolds toyed with the sugar packets. "I trusted him. But a lot of field officers end up this way. There's money and excitement and deals to be made. South America is like a drawer full of candy to a smart guy like Haden, and he's reached in and grabbed a handful."

Meredith didn't reply because she didn't know what to say, a vague sense of discontent marring the loyalty she had always shown her mentor. "I just don't know…."

Disapproval came into Reynolds's pale gray eyes.

"I thought I could depend on you, Meredith. I helped you a lot when you were on the official payroll. I got you where you are right now." He paused. "Surely you haven't forgotten that, have you?"

"I haven't forgotten anything you've done for me, Dean, and I never will," she said slowly. "But Jack is one of us—"

Dean's hand snaked out and captured her wrist before she could finish her sentence. She jerked her gaze to his face in surprise.

"He *was* but he isn't anymore." His voice turned fierce. His fingers squeezed painfully, then he released her and thumped the pile of black-and-white photos sitting on the tabletop between them. "*This* is what he's become and you have a duty to see that it doesn't go any further."

Meredith picked up the photographs he'd already shown her, her hands shaking in spite of herself. The first one was a long-distance shot of Jack Haden and two other men. Their faces were grainy but clear enough. She knew who the terrorists were. She moved on to the second one. It showed Haden on a busy street kissing a dark-haired woman. According to Reynolds, the woman was a courier for Al Balsair. Haden had one hand around her waist and the other at her neck. The kiss was a serious one and it'd instantly reminded Meredith of the kind *they'd* shared. She swallowed hard and pushed the memory aside, her eyes going to the third shot. Obviously caught at a party, Haden had been snapped standing beside a blond man and they were engrossed in a conversation, oblivious to all around them.

She tapped the last picture, distracting herself from the one before it. "Tell me again about this Prescott fellow…."

"He works for a telecommunications firm out of Boston called Redman Cellular," Reynolds said. "They're bidding on a job to install a series of towers down there for cell phone communication. It's easier than trying to get land lines to everyone. He went to Guatemala City two weeks ago. The last time his wife heard from him was three days later. Since then, not a word."

"Have you talked to anyone at Redman?"

"I've spoken with Prescott's boss several times."

"No mention of a ransom?"

"He said no. He's upset and worried, but at a loss to figure out what happened, or so he says. Everything seems normal on the surface."

"But…?"

"But Redman Cellular's name came through the system earlier this year with a yellow flag. The American companies that have contracts in the Latin quadrant are overworked and understaffed. They're desperate to hang on to their deals so they're sending people down there who aren't anything but warm bodies. They don't know what they're doing, but their presence makes the locals think something's getting done and it buys the companies more time."

"But in the meantime, all anyone employed by Redman needs is a legitimate work visa and they're free to travel between South America and North America. Regular round trips aren't out of line— they're expected."

"Exactly."

"Perfect setup for a mule."

"You got it."

Meredith shook her head in disgust. The bad guys made so much money here they had to have it physically transported to Latin America. The women and men who shuttled the money and goods back and forth were called mules. Lately, with all the advances that had been made in electronic eavesdropping, information and other pieces of intelligence were frequently hand-carried as well.

"He'd left his hotel in Guatemala City for Panajachel," Dean continued. "That's on Lake Atitlán. It's a big tourist destination, but he never arrived."

"Who contacted you about the case?"

"Someone at his hotel reported the incident and the Guatemala City police took it from there."

She leaned closer. "You don't generally deal with things at this level. Other than the flag on Redman Cellular, what makes Prescott so special?"

"Nothing," he said bluntly, "except that photograph right there." He pointed to the one showing Prescott talking to Haden. "That was taken right before he disappeared. They both 'happened' to be at the same party. A few days later, Prescott vanished."

She nudged the photo of Prescott to reveal the final one in the pile. It was a long shot of Jack Haden, sitting alone at a table outside a restaurant. Her fingers brushed the image of his face as if by accident, but the recollections that heated inside her were anything but casual.

Meredith spoke carefully. "Haden has always been well-liked at the Agency. I was surprised when I heard he'd transferred to Guatemala."

Reynolds studied her face. Meredith stared back calmly. She was confident he had no idea she and Haden had been lovers. No one had been better than the two of them at keeping secrets. Even from each other.

Especially from each other.

"I was surprised, too," Reynolds said finally. "I always thought Hades would close Langley down and turn out the lights after everyone else had gone."

She smiled without thinking at the nickname but her expression changed as Reynolds continued.

"I find it hard to believe he's involved in this whole mess, too, but he is. We have the photos and surveillance on the ground. His fingerprints were all over Prescott's room. You can confirm that with the police if you like. The rest of the information I've given you is confidential, of course. But if you want to double-check it..." His voice was stiff and defensive.

"That won't be necessary. You've shown me the photos. If you're sure, that's good enough for me."

"I've never been more positive of anything in my life. I wouldn't have called you if I'd had the slightest doubt."

"Where is he right now?"

"Guatemala City as far as I know. He hasn't been in the office for a couple of days, but he's still in the country. I would have heard if he'd left."

She sat quietly for a few seconds, then she asked the question she'd been holding back since Dean had called her two days before. "You have other ways to handle this." Her eyes locked on his. "Why me?"

"You're the best," he said without preamble. "And that's what I have to have."

She started to interrupt, but he stopped her with an uplifted hand.

"When Jack's disappearance comes to light— and it will—the investigation will be very thorough. The people in D.C. who work these kinds of details will turn Guatemala upside down trying to figure out what happened. I can't have any loose ends pointing back to me or, God forbid, the president." He shook his head, a look of disgust on his face. "Can you imagine what would happen if the press were to learn the U.S. president had sanctioned one of his own men? The Agency would be destroyed and no one would care that we'd saved ten thousand lives in the process." He stared at her without blinking. "You're the only person who can do this and do it right. If any mistakes are made, we'll *all* go down, the country included. You're the only person in the world I can trust to do this right."

His confidence in her was reassuring. For a minute, she felt as if her dad were sitting beside her. "And Prescott?"

He crumpled his coffee cup, the action holding a finality. "Prescott's a civilian. If something happens to him, it would be unfortunate, especially if he's innocent. Try to bring him back."

Her words came out with difficulty. "How do you want it to happen?"

"I don't really care," he said coolly. "But if I were you, I'd find out if Haden knows where Prescott is before you take care of…things. Other than that, it doesn't matter. You're the professional."

TELLING HER MENTOR she needed some time, Meredith left without giving Dean Reynolds a firm answer. She turned in her rental car at the airport, found her terminal and sat down, her thoughts a lot more convoluted than they had ever been before.

She'd loved working at the CIA and felt as if she'd been made for the job, but that had been the trouble, according to Reynolds. She'd been so good—"born to it," he'd said, "the kind of agent we get once in a lifetime"—it was felt her talents were being wasted at her post in D.C.

Still, she'd been surprised by Reynolds's support. The Agency was a place where it was every man for himself. Reynolds was an uptight, by-the-book patriot lawyer who'd been the Director of Operations for years. He'd survived four presidents, two wars and a terrorist attack at the CIA's headquarters eight miles outside downtown D.C. He didn't hand out favors easily.

At the conclusion of Meredith's third year, though, Reynolds had pulled her into his office and pushed a laptop computer across his desk to her. Open on the screen was a written report, the pages of which vanished after she read each one. In the corner there had been a drawing of a small black box. She'd understood what that meant at the end—when the words *Classification: Black Box* had flashed across the screen, then disappeared.

She'd had no idea there was a level of secrecy within the Agency designated as *black box*. A class so far above the others that it was described only as *silent.* When Dean had explained the protocol, she'd been speechless.

"You'll have to be fired from the Agency," he'd said. "And you will have to leave in disgrace. No one can ever know that the Operatives have the president's blessings. If anyone did find out—" He'd stopped abruptly and broken their eye contact. After a short pause, he'd continued. "If they find out, it would be bad, very bad, for all concerned."

In a daze of disbelief, she'd almost laughed out loud at that point, the old joke about "I could tell you but then I'd have to kill you" coming to her. One look at the older man's expression, however, had sent her amusement fleeing. She'd gone home and agonized over the opportunity but in the end, she'd agreed, the patriotism running through her too strong to resist the pull of performing a service this special for her country. She'd thrown in only one condition—she wanted her father's help. A former Navy intel man, he'd been quickly approved and even welcomed into the circle.

The Operatives had come together shortly after that. Handpicked by her father and cleared by Meredith, the three men on the team each had their speciality: Stratton O'Neil was a sniper. Jonathan Cruz used his hands. Armando Torres was a doctor, and no one understood exactly how he did what he did.

Meredith's weapon of choice was the knife.

They were assassins and only a handful of people knew it.

Of those, fewer still knew the whole truth: Every hit they'd ever made had been a sanctioned one, vetted and cleared by the president of the United States himself. The secret was buried so well that even the men on the team didn't know. At least, not officially. They'd guessed by now, she was sure, but nothing had ever been said about their status.

Haden had not been included in the group who knew these facts. He thought the Operatives were mercenaries, plain and simple. A year or so after she'd been "fired," she'd run into him at Heathrow. He'd been on his way to the Sudan and she'd been going to Hong Kong. She'd wanted desperately to avoid him, but escape had been out of the question. He'd started straight for her the second he'd seen her.

"I hear you've a very rich woman," he said without preamble.

"I make a living."

His eyes had turned hard and glittery. "A real killing?"

The double entendre had left her trembling on the inside but she'd smiled. "You could say that."

He'd shaken his head in disgust and walked away. Watching him leave, Meredith had understood, in a way she hadn't before then, that her former life was truly over. All she had left was her job. Everything else had been sacrificed for her country.

With the motivation of a higher purpose guiding their actions, the Operatives had proceeded to make the world a safer place. She'd never felt a moment's doubt about their goals until today when she'd looked in Dean Reynolds's eyes and heard him say Jack Haden's name.

Watching a 747 angle into its berth twenty feet from where she sat, she sighed heavily and admitted to the hesitation she'd felt during her meeting with Dean. She didn't doubt his intel but something just didn't feel right.

Her doubts plagued her the whole flight home. She knew the Miami airport better than she knew her own backyard but when she got in late that night, she got lost pulling out of the parking lot. Finally, she found the right road and she headed home.

Turning into her driveway at midnight, Meredith parked inside the garage and lowered the door. When it was completely down, she unlocked the car and retrieved her overnight bag from the trunk. Once inside, she flicked on the lights and turned off her burglar alarm, then she went through the house with her blade at her side. Her actions were routine but they weren't taken lightly. A price had been on her head for years.

She finished her check and came back to the kitchen. Laying her knife on the countertop where her cell phone already rested, she leaned her hip against the cabinet and closed her eyes, her mind occupied with the images and sensations Dean's proposition had brought back to her.

Haden's face in the dark, his body, toned and hard, the touch of his fingers along her jaw. She'd hidden her memories beneath a layer of protective armor after their breakup, but Dean's words had ripped that shield right off.

She'd given up everything for her country; the possibility of a family and a husband, not to mention children, were not in her future and they never would be. She'd traded those things for adrenaline and power—life-and-death power—and it was way too late to go back and make changes.

If she'd ever had a chance at having any of those things, it would have been with Haden, though. He'd been wild, but under the craziness there had been a rock-solid man she'd come to care for more than she'd expected. More than anyone she'd ever cared for before—or since. He'd been special and rare—one of those guys who caught you unaware when you'd decided no one else could possibly surprise you.

For a single second she wanted to walk away and ignore the decision she'd wrestled with for the past five hours, but she knew that wasn't a real option.

If Reynolds wanted Haden dead, it was going to happen.

If she didn't take the job, then someone else would. Haden would fall ill. Or get hit by a car. Or drown in a pool.

He was a dead man walking.

Before she could think about it any more, she picked up her cell phone and dialed. It was almost 1:00 a.m. but Dean Reynolds answered on the second ring, his voice deep, his manner alert. "Reynolds here."

"I'll call you when I get there," she said. "Don't try to contact me. You won't be able to." She hung up before he could ask any questions.

CHAPTER TWO

SHE HIT THE END BUTTON then dialed a second number. It was an hour earlier in Peru where Armando Torres lived, but he answered as quickly as Dean Reynolds had.

"I'm taking some time off," she said. "I thought I should let you know."

"That's good." His calm acceptance of her announcement was typical. Nothing ruffled Armando, except his new wife. They'd met when she'd come to his clinic near Machu Picchu in search of some answers to questions from her past. He'd helped her find them and they'd fallen in love in the process. "Are you going somewhere warm where the water is blue and the drinks are cold?"

"I'm going to Guatemala," she answered. "Does that count?"

A small silence built. "Since there is no other reason to visit that godforsaken country, I must assume you're an aficionado of antiquities and I didn't know it."

"I'm not, but a friend of mine is having some problems. I'm going down there to see if I can help."

"You have a friend besides Julia?" His voice lightened. "I don't believe it!"

Meredith chuckled. Armando had met her best friend, Julia Vandamme when she and Jonathan Cruz had married a short time ago. Cruz had saved Julia from a very bad situation in Colombia before stealing her heart.

"This is a friend I don't usually claim, but I think he's gotten himself into some trouble. I can't walk away."

Armando's voice stayed neutral. "Trouble in Guatemala can be deadly. It's not a nice place."

"That's why I wanted you to know where I'll be. Whatever happens, it won't be easy."

"Maybe you should send Stratton instead?"

Stratton O'Neil had left the Operatives, but he still helped them out on occasion. He was very good in tricky situations.

"I'd like to send him," she said now, "but this is something I have to do."

"Are you sure?"

She looked out to the courtyard where a late night shower had left diamonds glittering on the leaves of the ferns. All her windows faced the courtyard. There were no openings to the street and the world beyond, a metaphor for her life, she'd often thought.

"I don't really like Guatemala," she mused. "I don't understand the country but yes, I'm sure. I don't have a choice."

"Meredith, *por favor,* we always have choices. You know that better than anyone," he chided her gently. "You have had to make some hard ones yourself."

"You have, too, my friend."

"Maybe so, but that is life, eh?"

"I suppose."

He hesitated, as polite as ever, but his concern overrode his reserve. "If you have a lack of enthusiasm about this situation, perhaps it is best to reconsider?"

"I've already committed myself. That isn't an option."

"Which only serves to make my point."

"You're right," she said. "But I said I'd help."

"I understand," he conceded. "Some obligations must be met, regardless of their cost."

"Thanks for listening. You're a good friend, Armando."

"Return the favor by staying safe."

"I'll do my best."

THE RAINY SEASON WAS supposed to stop at the end of May but someone had forgotten to tell Mother Nature. Water glistened in black puddles when Meredith stepped outside the terminal at La Aurora International in Guatemala City the following night, a cool breeze accompanying the errant drips still falling from the edge of the roof. She pulled her sweater close as she passed five men in military garb. They each carried an automatic weapon slung casually over the shoulder and they watched Meredith as she headed toward the waiting taxis, a single light bag in her hand.

The president of Guatemala had been overthrown in the late fifties and since that time, the government, such as it was, had been under the command of a parade of generals and dictators, each more corrupt than the previous. In the eighties, the country had turned into a killing field. Things had gotten better in the late 90s, but no one forgot what it had been like and most expected it would return. The poverty was staggering.

The address she gave the taxi driver was in the Zona Viva, an area of town comprised of restaurants and hotels with plenty of upscale houses as well. Traffic was heavy despite the lateness of the hour but they got there eventually. She tipped the driver an amount reasonable enough to be acceptable but not enough to be remembered, then climbed out of the car in front of a hotel. Walking briskly, she lost herself in the crowd of pedestrians coming toward her. Four blocks later, she turned south. The commercial buildings became villas and fifteen minutes after that, she stopped and tapped twice on a wooden fence. A gate, unseen until that point, swung back, a slice of light spilling out from behind it to the darkened sidewalk. Meredith slid inside and the lock clicked behind her.

She'd never been in this particular house but it was so similar to the ones she always used that she barely noticed its comfortable furniture or generous rooms. The only thing she cared about was privacy and anonymity. Having to worry about someone recognizing her was the last thing she wanted. She made a quick check of the windows and doors, then had an even quicker conversation with the man who'd opened the gate. He knew better than to ask any questions and twenty minutes after she'd arrived, Meredith was settled in. The maps she'd requested were on the kitchen table. She made herself a cup of coffee and sat down with the phone.

The first number she dialed was Cipriano Barrisito's. She'd called him from the States before leaving and told him what she needed. She listened to the phone ring and thought about the tasks that faced her.

His voice was slick and deep when he answered. He was a fixer, a man who hung on the edges of both good and bad, doing whatever needed to be done for whoever had the money. *"¿Bueno?"*

"It's me," she said. "I'm here."

"That's good. Was your journey a smooth one?"

"I'm still in one piece," she said. "Will I see you tonight?"

"Actually, I'm sending my cousin, Rosario. When I told the family that I needed some information of a certain type, she came to me." He laughed. "You know how it works. She has a friend, who has a friend, who has a friend…."

Barrisito's "family" consisted of a dozen or so hookers he ran in the center of town. They represented only one facet of his organization, but when he needed to know something, the women were where he went first.

Meredith murmured her assent, but when he spoke again, his tone was guarded and uncertain, a fact that made her nervous. "I'm not sure we can shed any light on the problem, though."

She hid her reaction by mock surprise. "Your family is always so friendly and helpful, *mi amigo*. I find that hard to believe. What are you saying?"

"The situation is…fluid, as you like to say in the north. The friend you inquired about seems to be out of town at the moment. Perhaps he's joined the other gentleman you mentioned?"

As was her way, Meredith had explained as little as possible when she'd called Cipri earlier. She needed to locate Brad Prescott, she'd said, and Jack Haden might be able to help. Was he around?

"They're *both* out of pocket now?" she asked.

"That seems to be the case," Barrisito said. "I may have a handle on where they went, but like I said, I'm not sure at this point."

"How long has my friend been gone?"

"That, I don't know. All I do know is that he didn't turn up for work yesterday or today. I may learn more within the next hour. If I do, Cousin Rosario will tell you when you see her."

They said their goodbyes, Meredith's concern rising over this latest turn of events. Where in the hell was Haden? Had he gone back to the States? For half a second, she thought of calling Reynolds to see what he knew, but in the end, she decided to stick with her original plan.

A little after eleven, she headed back to the business district. The bar was easy to find, its blaring techno pop competing with the even louder salsa music coming from the place next door. She sat down near the door and waited. Five minutes later Cousin Rosario slipped into the empty seat across the table. Her skimpy yellow blouse and cheap black skirt advertised her work, her hard face and made-up eyes, further confirmation. They chatted in Spanish and acted as if they'd known each other forever, checking on nonexistent relatives and verifying their identities in the process. After sharing a plate of tapas they got up and left together, heading down a busy side street to a small *parque*.

They made their way to a bench under a huge mahogany tree. It was late and getting later but the *parque* was still fairly full, a family with five children sitting in the grass nearby, their innocent laughter totally incongruent with the conversation the two women were about to have.

Meredith spoke first. "So what do you know?"

The woman was accustomed to people in a hurry. She took no notice of Meredith's rush.

"Cipri told me you're looking for someone. A gringo… I came because I have a friend who works up north. By Lake Ati. She goes to this place once a week. It's like a prison but it isn't."

"What do you mean it's 'like' a prison?"

The woman shrugged. "It's not an official place, you know? The men, they're locked up, okay? But the guards, they let the women in easy, no hassle like the *policia* would give them. All they want is something in return. They get *la mordida*—just a little money, not big like the police—then the women, they do their jobs and leave. No problems." She explained the layout of the compound, her hands moving gracefully.

"Who puts the men there?" Meredith asked when she finished. "Who runs the place?"

The woman looked at her blankly. If she knew, she wasn't telling.

"All right," Meredith said impatiently. "So there's two gringos there, correct? What do they look like—"

"No." The hooker interrupted. "Not two. My friend, she say nothing about two. There was only one. One man. Cipri, he asked me that, too, but *hay sólo uno.*"

The uneasiness that had started during Meredith's conversation with Barrisito raised another notch. Just as he'd pointed out, situations like this *were* always changing, but Meredith had come down here believing Prescott was the only MIA. Then Barrisito had told her Haden was gone, too.

Now she was back to one man?

"Does this gringo have a name?" she asked.

"They call him *Árabe.*"

"The Arab?" Meredith frowned in confusion. She'd always thought of Haden as a younger version of Nick Nolte in his good days. Bright blue eyes, white-blond hair, broad shoulders, a gravelly voice. There was no way anyone would confuse him with an Arab. If the man in prison was called the Arab, he couldn't be Haden. At the same time, the picture Dean had given her of Brad Prescott had shown a fairly young man with light hair and green eyes. His features hadn't been dark enough to give the impression of a Middle Eastern heritage, but maybe his skin could have burnished under the Mayan sun. "*Is* he Arab?" she asked.

The woman shrugged again, this time with a casualness that tried Meredith's patience. "I don't know."

"What does he look like?"

"I don't know."

"Does he speak English?"

"I don't know. Look, are you gonna pay me now? I have to get my money—"

Meredith waited a beat, then she leaned closer, her voice a fraction lower, her face expressionless. "I want you to try real hard to remember what your friend told you," she said quietly. "So far, I haven't heard anything that's worth a single quetzal, much less the hundred dollars you demanded."

The woman inched backward on the bench as a soft drizzle began. The rain hit the leaves on the tree that sheltered them. "I—I don't know what else to tell you. That's all she said."

"Try harder," Meredith pressed. "What color is his hair? What color are his eyes? Which cell was he in?"

"I—I don't know—" She stopped abruptly, her hand going to the base of her neck. "No, no…she did say something about his eyes, I remember now."

Meredith waited.

"My friend, she say they were *vacíe*."

"Empty?"

"*Sí, sí.* That's right. Emtie, yes." She stood and held her hands up, palms out. "That's all I know, *señorita*. There's nothing more, I promise." A second later, she was gone.

For another ten minutes, Meredith sat under the tree in the falling rain and considered her options. Then she got up and started walking.

Her feet didn't head the direction she ordered them to, though. They started down *Calle 6b* and fifteen minutes later, she found herself outside Jack Haden's home.

CHAPTER THREE

STANDING IN THE SHADOWS across the street, Meredith stared at the house then closed her eyes for half a second. She could envision Haden inside, tracing the patterns on tiled floors with his toes, trailing his fingers over the polished wood banisters, leaning against the stuccoed wall. Haden was the kind of guy who liked to touch things he was familiar with— it gave him a sense of comfort, she'd decided after watching him one day. He liked to reassure himself that he was where he thought he was and the things around him were his own. He'd touched her that way, too.

She opened her eyes and studied the home a little closer. Built like the others around it, nothing about the building stood out, which was probably one of the reasons it appealed to him. Two stories with a red tiled roof, the place was surrounded by a painted wall that looked to be about ten feet tall. The top of it was decorated with bits of colored broken glass, the jagged edges pointing straight up. Anyone trying to boost themselves over would end up with a bloody gash across the palm.

A black iron gate was set in the stucco and through the bars, she could see a small garden. The front door opened to the patio. There was no garage and reminding her of her own home, all the windows faced the interior courtyard. A dim reflection ricocheted off the glass of the nearest one but there were no lights on inside.

She glanced down the street. Haden could have afforded a better *colonia,* but he'd obviously chosen this one for a reason. She wondered if his selection had had anything to do with the lack of vehicles parked outside. If your neighbors were too poor to have cars, then you heard one when it came down the street in the middle of the night. Here, in times past, the sound of a car drawing near after dark was one people dreaded. They'd lock their doors and hide, praying no one would knock. In the morning, they'd get up and surreptitiously check their neighbors to see who had been taken away.

Things were supposed to better now, but who could say for sure? Haden would have been cautious regardless.

She edged down the *calle* toward a patch of darkness that spread all the way across the street, then she crossed, the smell of fried tortillas filling the air, the sound of a distant radio coming with it.

She'd planned on walking by and nothing more, but when she was even with the gate, she couldn't resist. Her hand reached out and touched one of the bars and the whole thing drifted backward without a sound.

She froze.

Haden would have never left the gate open if he'd gone out of town and if he *was* home, he would have been even more careful about checking it.

She looked over her shoulder in both directions, then glided inside the walled enclosure, her steps muted. No moon lit the sky but there was enough ambient light to make out the bushes and plants in pots around a central fountain. Edging around the perimeter, she headed for a door set between two of the windows.

The taste of fear filled her dry mouth and suddenly she realized her knife was in her hand. She didn't remember pulling the weapon from her boot but her fingers were wrapped around it so she must have. When she reached the door, she used the tip of the blade to press against the wood and swing it open. The slab of heavy mahogany complied with a soft creak.

She wished it had stayed shut.

The room before her had been destroyed. There were holes in the stucco where things had been thrown and most of the furniture was upside down.

A brown couch lay on its side, its ripped cushions scattered from one end of the room to the other. Two small chairs had been pushed over, too, their arms sticking uselessly into the air. The coffee table was the same way, but it only had three legs. One had been broken off with a savagery that made her swallow, a jagged piece of wood sticking out from the frame like a broken bone. The leg that had been ripped off lay near the shattered television set. The tip had been dipped in something brown and sticky. Her eyes backtracked the trail leading up to it. The line was long and ropy. On the wall where it began was a smeared handprint.

She stepped inside the room, avoiding a stain on the tile floor at the threshold to close the door behind her. Standing quietly, she listened to the flies buzz nearby, then she moved down the hallway on her left in a quick but silent stride. Within minutes, she knew the house was empty.

She returned to the den and surveyed the destruction again. Whatever had happened here had happened several days before, but the echoes of violence left behind could still be felt. Suppressing a shudder, Meredith tried to concentrate but it was almost impossible. Death had been here.

The heavy silence was broken with the incongruent sound of a baby crying. Meredith blinked twice, then realized the noise was coming from next door.

She glanced at the house in time to see a light come on behind a open window on the second floor. Had they seen anything? Had they heard anything? The outline of a small lamp wavered behind a filmy curtain. It threw enough illumination over the stucco fence that when she turned back to the den, some of the details she'd missed before came into clearer view.

The first thing she noticed was the wall behind the front door. The pale yellow paint was marked with the scuff of a shoe. It looked as if someone had stood there and rested a boot against the stucco. She imagined the scene—the door slowly opening, the person behind makes the first strike, the beating ensues. Who had been waiting? Who had walked inside?

She picked her way through the debris to the other side of the room. Along with everything else, there were five cigarette butts scattered in the mess, all of them Payasos, the local Guatemalan brand. Kneeling down she stilled. Haden didn't smoke. Acting on instinct, she lifted them one by one with the end of her knife and, ripping a page from a nearby book, wrapped the cigarettes up in the paper before dropping the packet into her pocket. She didn't know what the cigarettes might tell her later, but information was information and years of training wouldn't let her ignore it.

She studied the bookshelves. They had obviously been bumped during the struggle, books and photos tumbling out of their shelves to the floor beneath. Something silver glinted in the light but before she could tell what it was, the room went dark again. The baby had gone silent, she realized, and the neighbor had doused his lamp.

Stepping closer, she bent down anyway and dug through the debris with the edge of her knife. She had to push aside a heavy candle and then move a travel book on Machu Picchu, but she finally reached the thing that had caught her attention.

It was a picture frame, she realized. And it held a photograph of her.

RETURNING TO THE SAFE HOUSE, Meredith called Cipriano Barrisito immediately. The need to rush was long past—the blood had been shed days ago—but she couldn't hold back her sense of urgency.

He answered as before, right on the third ring. "Did everything go as you wanted?"

"Not exactly," she said. "My friend may have a bigger problem than I first thought. I need you to go to his barrio and ask some questions."

"*Dígame.*"

She gave him the address of Haden's neighbor then said, "Send someone over there right now. They have a young child and they probably don't sleep too soundly. I want to know if they heard any…noise at the house next door." She took a sip of the drink she'd poured for herself before grabbing the phone. "It would have happened over the last two days, maybe three."

Barrisito hesitated. "What would this unusual sound have been?"

"Just ask them. When you find out, call me back."

She was on her second drink when the phone rang, its strident sound making her jerk so hard, a splash of tomato juice and vodka spilled from her glass onto her blouse. The stain reminded her of the ones she'd seen in Haden's house.

"Night before last, they heard a car on the street behind them," Barrisito confirmed. "Then men talking loudly."

"How many?"

"At least two, maybe three. They weren't sure."

"Did they recognize anyone?"

"No."

"What happened?"

"A fight, but they ignored it," he said. "This is Guatemala. You don't stick your nose where it doesn't belong. It might get chopped off."

"How long did it last?"

"Not long." He paused. "When it was over, they said one man left the house and walked away. They saw no one else after that and they've seen no one since." He spoke quietly. "If your friend was somehow taken to the place my cousin told you about, I would leave this alone."

"I don't think that's him," she said quietly, the feeling she'd had at Haden's returning. Death had been in there. She'd felt it. "Rosario said only one gringo was there. I doubt that it's Haden. It may be Brad Prescott, though."

"Whoever he is, leave him be. Fidel Menchez controls everything in that part of the country. Everything between Guatemala and Mexico. And he's not a pleasant man."

She tried to focus. "Tell me more."

"There's nothing more to tell. For a small fee, he will guarantee safe passage for the other men's couriers who must pass through his area but if you do not pay, you end up in his prison."

"Is there no way out?"

"I've heard of bribes helping, but the price, it is too high for most."

"How big is this place? Are there that many couriers going back and forth?"

"He has other 'prisoners' as well. For his friends—his *paying* friends—Menchez will help out with someone who needs to be 'disappeared.' They go in, they don't come out."

"Why not just kill them?"

"Killing would be easier," Barrisito conceded,

"but you have to remember where you are. This is Guatemala. Everything can be used as a bargaining chip. One never knows when a trade can be made. Why waste the bullet?"

Meredith's mind spun as he talked, her plan coalescing quickly, the seed for it having already been planted the minute the hooker had mentioned her friend's visit to the prison.

"You're *loca*," he said after Meredith explained what she wanted to do. "These people are not the kind you are accustomed to dealing with. They have no honor. You do not understand."

"I've worked with their ilk before."

"I do not think so," he said. "If you had, you would not be around to tell about it."

"I can handle myself," she said grimly. "You just hold up your end. That's all you need to worry about."

She took a bath and went to bed but the sun came up a few hours later and found her still awake, thoughts of Haden plaguing her. In her heart, she knew he was dead and the heaviness that weighed her down was both shocking and unexpected. She analyzed her reaction further, her emotions rising to the surface. The idea of Haden being gone left her completely adrift, but at the same time, she felt a twisted relief over the fact that she hadn't been the one to cause the situation. She shook her head in total confusion. What the hell was wrong with her?

Through the chaos one thought registered. If Haden and Prescott *had* been working together, then maybe Brad Prescott might know what had really happened at Haden's home. She coudn't leave without knowing the truth.

Turning her mind away from her thoughts, Meredith got out of bed and made some notes about what Barrisito's hooker had told her. When a glance at her watch told her the market had opened, she made a quick trip to one of the boutiques and then stopped at a postal service. After filling out all the forms and sealing up the cigarette butts she'd retrieved from Haden's house, she printed the address on the front of the lab she used in D.C. The butts might reveal nothing, but the chance they might reveal something was too great to ignore.

After returning to the house, she packed the clothing she'd bought into a small bag she found inside one of the closets, leaving the rest of her personal items in place. If things went the way she planned, she would be back during the early hours of Saturday morning and on a plane to Houston the following afternoon.

The clock chimed noon when she locked the house and left. The tote on one shoulder, her purse on the other, she walked briskly down the narrow street going the opposite direction she had the night before. In a matter of minutes she was on a busy commercial street. She crossed it twice, then finally decided on a particular cab. As they headed for Zona 8, the passing buildings turned bleaker and the streets narrower. The driver pulled up to the bus station and Meredith paid him, climbing out with one eye on her surroundings. The sun had come out and it was steamy, the smell of dust and smoke heavy all around. There was always something burning in Guatemala City. She entered the bus station and the haze actually seemed stronger inside.

Five hours later she got off the bus in Huehuet-enango.

She went into the nearest bathroom and took off the jeans and T-shirt she'd traveled in, replacing them with the short skirt and tight halter she'd bought earlier that morning. Lining her eyes with a dark pencil, she added another layer of mascara, then pulled her hair to one side with a wide rubber band. She took her shoes from the bag last of all. They were custom-made heels; the sole was as thin as a wafer and so was the blade it concealed. She checked the edge and handle carefully and then slipped the weapon back into its hidden compartment.

Judging from the looks she got when she came out, her transformation was a good one. She hoped the guards at the prison would think so, too, but her thoughts were interrupted as a man approached her.

He appeared familiar, then she remembered that Barrisito had told her he was sending his brother to meet her. The dark eyes that met hers were a mirror image of the man who'd warned her against coming.

His gaze went over her body then came back to her face. "Do you know what you're doing?"

He was as outspoken as his brother. "I can take care of myself," she said. "You just get me in."

He led her to his vehicle in silence, their conversation over. A few minutes later he pulled up in front of a small run-down hotel. A fountain bubbled quietly in the courtyard beside the street and the walls were covered with a thick green vine but nothing could hide the air of seedy despair that hung over it. A group of women were huddled next to a waiting van and they looked up as Barrisito's brother pulled his SUV up to the curb.

"That's them," he said.

Meredith ran her eyes over the scantily clad women. She would have known who they were without his input.

"I'll call you as soon as I can." She turned back to the man beside her. "Don't be late. Will this be the vehicle?"

"No, this is *my* car. I'll have another one for you."

"Make sure it's gassed up. I don't want to have to stop between here and Guatemala City. Do you know where to leave it?"

"*Sí, entiendo.*" His voice was sullen. He didn't like taking orders from a woman. "It will be there and the tank will be full. But you will not be needing it, I tell you the truth."

She paused, her hand on the latch. "And why is that?"

"You won't be coming back," he said smugly. "Menchez's men are no fools. They will know you are not who you say you are."

Leaning toward him, she held his gaze in the rearview mirror. "There's only one way they would know that and that's if you tell them. Should that happen, I'll return to make sure you don't do it again." She waited for her words to soak in. "Do you understand me?"

"I understand."

She didn't smile. "*Bueno.* I wouldn't want to have to give your brother bad news when I return to the city."

"I would not want that, either."

"Then keep your mouth shut," she said, her voice hard. "And have my car waiting."

THE WOMEN DIDN'T greet Meredith. They were experienced enough, if not old enough, to know it was best to ignore her. She represented the unknown and therefore, the dangerous. Still, she found herself wondering which one of them had told Barrisito's hooker about the gringo she'd seen. It wouldn't have hurt to have a friend in the group, but Meredith knew even better than they did that strangers were to be avoided.

The driver herded them into the van, passing out dirty black scarves as they climbed inside. Meredith watched as one by one, the women wrapped the rags around their eyes. She followed suit but when she saw the driver wasn't going to check she left hers loose enough to see through. The woman beside her did the same. They exchanged a quick look before the woman turned away, Meredith's impression of her forming quickly out of necessity. Bored and already jaded, she was probably in her thirties but she could just as easily have been nineteen or fifty, her dark, long hair and slanted eyes giving away little more than her Indian heritage.

The van took the main road out of town, then went north about three miles, the pavement giving way to a dirt-rutted road. Meredith noted the intersection then turned her eyes to the foliage outside the window. The farther they went, the thicker it became, the branches of the rubber trees leaning over and scraping the windows as if to ask for sanctuary from the endless jungle. The driver slowed after five long minutes then turned left sharply. The van ground to a halt shortly after that, the brakes' squeaky protest announcing their arrival.

The women pulled off their masks and their purses came out, the smell of cheap perfume filling the air as they sprayed their necks and reapplied their lipstick. When the van's door opened, they passed through it in a cloud of cloying sweetness and Max Factor.

Ten yards from the bus, a single guard stood beside a rusting metal fence while another one sat behind a rickety desk. The women presented their purses to one and their bodies to the other, each searched with a thoroughness that would have done the airport screeners back in the U.S.A. proud. Meredith's turn came up quickly.

The man's hands were rough and impersonal as he patted down her sides and hips then felt under her breasts. His breath was a mixture of stale beer and strong garlic. She let him do his job, then she stepped back and sucked in a lung full of air. He threw a comment over her shoulder to the man at the desk. His words were in Mam, a local dialect but the meaning was clear; she'd passed. She stared straight ahead like the novice she was supposed to be, moving only after he jerked his head for her to go on, switching to Spanish. *"Pase adelante."*

She stepped inside the prison and surveyed the grounds.

The description she'd gotten from the hooker had been accurate, she saw with relief. A fenced-in area opened out before her, the lot roughly forty-by-forty with a packed dirt floor and abandoned guard towers at either end. To her right was a cracked sidewalk lit by a row of bare lightbulbs hanging overhead. A half-dozen concrete benches were nearby, two broken-down picnic tables beside them. On the opposite side of the sidewalk was a small, open-air cinder-block building with peeling paint and four doors made of hanging fabric. An ancient fan sat on the crosspiece above each scrap of material, their blades rattling softly. This was where the women saw their clients.

She looked past the immediate area to the prison beyond. Behind another fence was a larger building that obviously contained the *celdas* and a second open area that looked like a soccer field. Men were filing into it slowly. The only guards she saw were the two behind her, but she assumed there were others nearby. There were no offices or administrative structures, in fact, there was nothing around that looked official in any way. Barrisito's explanation had been right on target.

When the visitors were all inside, the gate squeaked open at the other end of the compound and the prisoners spilled out into the courtyard. The women pushed forward and Meredith allowed them to carry her the same direction. The two groups met in the center of the dust-filled yard and chaos took over.

The prison population was made up mainly of locals and they were uniformly short—a taller individual, blond or otherwise, would stand out. Meredith's eyes scanned the crowd but she didn't have to look long. In the center of the group, a man wearing a white rag wrapped around his head caught her attention, one part of the puzzle falling into place. He wasn't an Arab but his makeshift ghutra had earned him the nickname. Her eyes dropped to his face and she sucked in a breath of horror.

The man was a mess. Covered in bruises and cuts, his skin was puffy and stretched, one eye so swollen it was completely closed, the other one a narrow slit. He hadn't been trying for a political statement with the dirty white towel—he'd simply wrapped himself up in an effort to hold the pieces together. Her eyes skipped over the details because she didn't want to look any closer, but a long ragged gash down one cheek stood out and she couldn't ignore it; the open wound was hot and ugly. She winced at the thought of the pain he must feel, sympathy passing through her.

There was no resemblance between the man before her and the photo of Brad Prescott. Then again, she thought with pity, this poor bastard's own mother wouldn't have known who he was.

Meredith took a deep breath and pushed her way toward him.

CHAPTER FOUR

SHE DIDN'T RECOGNIZE HIM.

Disbelief mixing with confusion, Haden watched Meredith Santera approach him, determination pulling her mouth into a single line, her steps quick and dogged. Without even looking at him, she grabbed his hand, pivoted and dragged him behind her, small puffs of dust rising from their steps as she hurried to beat the others to the *casitas*.

He was battered, but his brain was still working and he realized instantly that Meredith's appearance was not a good thing.

As he had the thought, though, Haden found his eyes dropping to her tight skirt and the curves it hugged that he'd once known so intimately. In total amazement, he felt himself respond to her, the situation so bizarre, he almost laughed out loud. He'd been beat to shit and now Meredith was here to finish the job and all he could think about was getting into her pants.

She flicked the curtain back and entered the room, pulling him in with her.

"We only have ten minutes." She threw a look over her shoulder and began to unbutton her blouse, her voice low and urgent. "Take off your clothes and get on the mattress. We have to make this look good or they'll get suspicious."

When he didn't move, she yanked him to her and began to unzip his pants. "C'mon, c'mon. We don't have much time. I know you're hurt but work with me, okay?"

Before he could respond, his jeans were halfway to his knees. She gave him a little push and he fell against the filthy mattress behind him. She was on top of him a moment later, her skirt hiked to her waist, her warm thighs straddling his.

"I'm going to create a diversion." Bending over to speak in his ear, she moved closer, her hair forming a curtain around them that felt like silk and smelled like heaven. "All you need to do is move when I tell you. Don't do anything else and for God's sake, don't argue with me." Her legs tightened as she continued, her resolve obvious. She threw back her head and moaned convincingly, then leaned down to his ear once more time. "I know what I'm doing, all right? Don't fight me and everything will be fine."

Outside someone snickered and Haden leaned to one side to look past Meredith. One of the guards stood beside the curtain, his hot gaze trained on Meredith's rear, his wet lips glistening under the yellow lights hung overhead.

Following his stare, Meredith glanced over her shoulder and she smiled. Then she began to move up and down, her hips mocking the rhythm she and Haden had shared dozens of times before, her moans growing louder. Tossing her hair in a gesture that stopped his breath, she put on a show that had him convinced, the expression of ecstasy on her face so believable it made him wonder about the times when her satisfaction was supposed to have been genuine. She continued with the show until the guard moved on.

Then she glanced down and her mouth fell open. His eyes tracked her stare and he saw what she'd seen.

He still had the tattoo.

Her eyes flew to his face, recognition dawning. "Oh, my God! Haden? Is that you? I didn't expect—"

Before she could finish, a scream filled the courtyard and all hell broke loose.

HADEN BUCKED Meredith off and jumped to his feet, the noise outside growing louder by the minute. She landed on the floor in a daze. She'd been expecting Brad Prescott, but she hadn't gotten him. Yet except for the tattoo, the man standing above her bore no resemblance to anyone she'd ever known, and that included Jack Haden.

But that's who he was and she knew it for a fact.

They'd gotten matching tattoos one night when alcohol had overtaken what little good sense they'd had left. She'd had hers removed the next day. Haden had laughed and said he was keeping his—and he obviously had, the small gold star still gleaming on his hipbone.

He jerked up his pants, suspicion filling his distorted features. "Who were you expecting, Meredith? You seem a little surprised."

She gaped at him a moment longer, then the chaos outside intruded again. She'd had a diversion planned, but whatever was happening couldn't be a part of it—it was way too soon. She'd told Barrisito's brother to wait until she'd come out of the shack and given him the signal.

Before she could answer, Haden grabbed her arm and hauled her to her feet. "Forget it—you can tell me later! We need to get the hell out of here. This might be our only chance!"

"No!" She twisted away and reached for her shoe, slipping the knife from the sole and hiding it in her waistband. "I have a plan—it's already in place. A fight's going to break out and then—"

He looked at her as if she'd lost her mind. "Screw your plan! This is it! We're leaving now!"

Without waiting, he gripped her arm again, then pulled her toward the doorway, her blouse half-on, her skirt still up around her waist. She yanked the garment down, then managed to bend over and snag her shoes. She got one on, then hopped a step and slipped on the other.

They were swallowed by the crowd the second they stepped outside. If Haden hadn't had the hold on her hand that he did, they would have been torn apart. Thrusting and shoving, screaming and yelling, the inmates were throwing punches and going wild, some already climbing up the fence behind the guard shack.

"This way!" Haden yelled at her and pointed over the prisoners who swirled around them. "The gate's on the south side of the complex—"

"No! Not that way!" She turned in a different direction. "We have to go this way! Over here!"

He couldn't hear her, or if he did, he ignored her. Using his battered body as a shield, he headed the way he'd indicated, dragging her behind him. Meredith tried to restrain him but her efforts were useless. The crowd was gaining momentum and now they were adding pressure from behind. Even if they'd wanted to, changing course became impossible.

They were almost to the fence when someone shrieked to Meredith's right. She jerked her head toward the sound and caught a glance of the woman who'd been sitting by her on the bus, her hand outstretched to Meredith's, her eyes two wells of terror. Meredith cried out and stopped, but Haden kept going and their linked hands were torn apart. The prostitute went down, her body falling under the inmates' boots as they surged toward the gate. Screaming, hands flailing, Meredith battled the wave of men to get back to the woman, but she didn't have a chance. She'd planned for a simple prison break, not a riot, now she couldn't help herself, much less anyone else.

She had to regain control and focus. She had a job to do.

A second later, a blow from behind knocked Meredith's breath from her chest. She stumbled and fell to one knee. The mob swelled and she pitched forward, but a hand reached out and heaved her up, saving her from sharing the other woman's fate. She looked up to see Haden's face. Then she was on her feet, and they were fighting through the crowd once more.

They made it to the fence a few minutes after that. Haden pushed her ahead of him and held the crowd back with his body, his hands stretched above her head where he gripped the rusty metal link. She gulped for air as he yelled something. She couldn't hear him and shook her head. Then he tilted his head and she understood. The guard who'd searched her was to their right. Standing before the gate, he was swinging his sap wildly but losing ground with every strike, the number of the now-crazed inmates too many to combat.

They were almost to the gate when Meredith

pulled her knife from the waistband of her skirt. She *had* to act now; she had no other choice.

A second later, they were by the prison guard's side. Taller than the man by a good six inches, Haden ducked closer as the guard's arm swung back. When he brought the sap down again, Haden grabbed the man's hand and twisted it backward, lifting it up at the very same time.

His whole left side was exposed. All Meredith had to do was take one step and thrust her knife.

A second later that's exactly what she did.

But it wasn't the guard she aimed for.

HADEN JUMPED and the knife missed him by an inch.

His startled eyes locked with Meredith's in the millisecond that followed and he read his fate in those dark-brown depths. Before he could react, an inmate came from behind and got between them, the fence finally falling down as the crowd pushed past the gate the guard had been trying to protect.

Haden dashed for the jungle without a backward look.

MEREDITH SHOT from the pack of stumbling inmates like a racehorse given its head but by the time she reached the clearing's edge, Haden had vanished. She plunged into the darkness anyway, a thousand scenarios flashing inside her head as to what would happen next. Her chances of finding him were good—he was already weak so he wouldn't get far—but she chastised herself regardless, the problem one that she shouldn't even have had to face.

What the hell had happened back there? How on earth could she have missed? Once her knife was out of its sheath, she never failed to hit her target. *Never.*

As she ran, she listed her excuses: the guard's movement had thrown her off, Haden had known she would try, the stars weren't lined up properly... In the end, she decided with disgust it didn't matter why she hadn't hit him. She'd botched things and that was all that counted.

She plunged deeper and deeper into the undergrowth until she pulled herself up short, her breath coming in quick bursts of frustration. This wasn't the way to get the job done. She was panicking and panic never got you anywhere. She had to pull herself together and come up with a plan. Bending over, she drew several deep breaths and tried to calm herself, but her brain wouldn't cooperate. She kept remembering one frightening image after another— the guard's horrified gaze merging with the terrified prostitute's eyes, her wide stare morphing into Haden's when he'd seen the knife in her hand.

Meredith bit back a curse and shook her head. What the hell had she been thinking? Why hadn't she handled the situation in the *casita* when she'd realized who he was? If she'd been prepared, she would have ditched the strategy she'd worked out and used the riot to her advantage, figuring out later how to escape and what to do with the body. She continued to berate herself but the truth didn't change. She'd screwed up. Big time.

Because she'd already decided he was dead.

Since the moment she'd walked into Haden's house, she'd assumed that was the case. There had been too much blood. Too much gore. She'd expected the man in the prison to be Brad Prescott. She remembered her feelings at seeing Haden's bloody home and everything clicked; she'd been *counting* on him being dead, she realized with a start.

Cursing out loud, she straightened and thought of her father, the sound of his voice echoing in the back of her mind. *Calm down. Clear your brain. Concentrate!*

Wiping her forehead, she blinked and listened to the imaginary advice. This wasn't the time or the place to figure out where she'd gone wrong. She needed to concentrate on what was in front of her and that's what she forced herself to do. After a second, her brain seemed to agree and settle down. Her task was really quite simple.

She had to find Haden.

Then she had to kill him.

Her senses on high alert, her body tense and ready, she headed into the brush, prepared to do just that.

HADEN SAT on a rotting log, the strength abandoning his legs as quickly as it'd come. He'd used every bit of energy he'd had to get this far but he hadn't gotten far enough. He could almost feel Meredith's hot breath behind him. She was good and she was fast. As soon as she recovered from the shock of missing him, she'd be right on his ass.

Shaky and queasy, Haden assessed his situation. Trying to escape was pointless; Meredith would never give up until she had him. The only reason he'd run was to give himself enough time to figure out how to handle her. If he could keep her off balance long enough, he might be able to understand what was happening before she managed to get that shank between his ribs.

"I didn't expect..."

Her shocked words when she'd realized who he was came back to him, and he filled in the part of the sentence she'd left unfinished. "I didn't expect *you...*" seemed obvious but if that was the case, then why had she tried to kill him? And who had she been looking for if not him?

The questions whirled in his mind, making as much sense as the howler monkeys overhead. After a bit, a single face emerged from his confusion and the more he thought about it, the more certain Haden became. Dean Reynolds was surely pulling these strings. The whole setup smelled like him, slick, smooth and not quite right.

Haden had tried to make Meredith see the truth when they'd been together, but she and the old man had always been thick. It seemed strange considering what she did for a living, but she'd always wanted to see the best in people. She was on the outside of the Agency now, but Haden wouldn't put anything past Reynolds. He'd manipulated Meredith back then and Haden knew it wouldn't bother the old bastard to use her now. Hell, Reynolds would pay off the Devil if it meant he could accomplish something he wanted.

Haden shifted his weight and a throbbing pain screamed through his head. He swayed, a wave of nausea overtaking him. He'd been in some tight spots, he thought as he struggled to stand, but it didn't get much worse than this. Holding on to the tree trunk behind him, he fought off his dizziness and amended his thought. Things could *always* get worse and they would…as soon as Meredith found him.

He took two steps forward then something behind him rustled in the underbrush. He froze and listened. A whisper of movement could be heard in the clearing just to his left. Haden smiled to himself then slipped silently to his right, his fingers gripping the vine he'd pulled down a few minutes before. He was glad to know there were some things he was still better at than Meredith. A few seconds later, he was behind her and she didn't have a clue. He took two more steps, then he was at her back.

He slipped his arm around her neck and pulled it tight against her throat.

To her credit, Meredith didn't cry out or make any sound at all. In fact, she went limp against him but Haden didn't fall for her trick. He tightened his hold and dragged her into the jungle, her back against his chest, the smell of her skin filling his senses to the point of overload.

She gripped his arm. "What are you doing?" Her voice was calm and even. "I followed you so I could help you, Haden. You don't have to do this. You need to get some medical attention."

"Yeah, sure. Help like yours I can do without." He jerked his arm against her throat. "We both know you aren't the Red Cross. You came here to kill someone, but you weren't expecting me and you tried anyway! I want to know who sent you and what the hell's going on."

Gritting his teeth against the pain the movement cost him, he wrapped the vine around her wrists, pulling it as tight as he could. He spoke over her shoulder as he tugged on it to make sure. "What's going on, Meredith?"

Her arms secured behind her, Meredith turned slowly. They were inches apart. "I don't know what you're talking about," she said, her eyes wide. "I was trying to get us out of there. I was aiming for the guard."

"The hell you were."

"It's the truth!"

He was weak and light-headed, but he jerked her closer and held on to the rope. "We both know what you do, Meredith. Don't screw with me."

"You wouldn't have said that a few years ago."

"You weren't a killer a few years ago," he said bluntly. "You were someone I could trust and I did. Things are different now."

"We do what we have to," she said. "That's how the world works."

"That's not how *my* world works," he said. "There are rules where I come from and you've broken them all." He tightened his jaw, a creeping blackness dimming the edges of his vision. The run into the jungle was taking its toll. "Just tell me why you're here, Meredith. Your services don't come cheaply so someone must be paying you a lot of money but you were obviously surprised to see me. Who *were* you looking for? And what does Dean Reynolds have to do with this?"

She looked him straight in the eye, her gaze cold.

"Go to hell, Haden," she said softly, her body still where it rested against his own. "I'm not telling you anything and you know better than to even ask."

He blinked, then a second wave of weakness hit him hard. He held his breath and rode it out. "You're going to tell me the truth," he insisted, "one way or another. Make it easy on yourself. I don't want to have to hurt you."

He heard her voice, but it seemed to come to him from a distant tunnel. "You couldn't hurt a mouse right now, Haden. Give it up…."

"I'm not giving up shit," he whispered. "I'll beat it out of you if I have to…." His threat faded into silence as he felt his knees buckle.

HADEN FELL to the jungle floor like a limp dish towel, taking her with him. If the situation had been slightly different, Meredith might have seen the humor in it, but right now all she could think about was getting things under control. The undergrowth cushioned their fall but he'd landed on top on her and her breath had left her chest in a whoosh. After a few seconds struggle, she wormed from beneath him and managed to get her hands untied. Two minutes later, she had their positions reversed, but her knots were much better. If he woke up before she got back, he wouldn't be going anywhere.

Heaving from the exertion of tying him, Meredith

headed back toward the prison to get her bearings, her footsteps noisy now that it no longer mattered. Within minutes she saw the lights and heard the voices talking in a mix of Spanish and Mam. A dozen men were saddling horses and getting ready, the animals sidestepping in nervous anticipation, the men nearby mimicking their mood. The ground outside what had been the prison perimeter was littered with casualties, some of the inmates dead, some wounded. The guards had simply killed the ones who'd been too slow to escape and now they were going to hunt down the rest. She glanced toward the horses. Their saddles had shotgun cases strapped to the sides.

She didn't wait to see more. Keeping to the shadows, she ran a path parallel to the road and tried to stay out of sight.

In twenty minutes, she was back at the intersection she'd noted from the bus. It felt like a lifetime, but little more than an hour had passed since the women had arrived.

Running back to the cutoff just past the road to the prison, she found what she'd been looking for. A battered blue Impala was parked just where she'd instructed Barrisito's brother to leave a vehicle. She waited and watched for a good five minutes but the road stayed empty, the area surrounding her dark and silent.

She wished her mind could be the same.

It was filled with Haden's words, though, shock still rippling over her at the way he'd spit out Dean Reynolds's name. How in the hell had he known about Reynolds's involvement in her task? She'd wondered at first if it'd been a lucky guess, but the way he'd spoken had triggered something inside her and all her previous doubt had returned in a flood.

The primary lesson her father had taught her was to always be sure. Be sure of her target. Be sure of her plan. Be sure of herself.

Every detail had to be checked and rechecked and then checked again.

She should have been sure killing Haden was the right thing to do.

And deep down, she hadn't been. She'd thought it was because she still had feelings for Haden, but what did the real reason matter? She had to be certain regardless and she wasn't…so she'd "missed" when she'd aimed for him, her body taking over from her mind to prevent a terrible mistake. The realization of what she'd done left her trembling but she *had* to pull herself together or the situation would get even more out of control. For a second longer, she struggled, then her equilibrium returned.

Stepping out of the darkness, she looked both ways then crossed the street. The car was unlocked.

She slipped inside, took the keys from the visor and started the engine, sending a look of satisfaction toward the gas gauge that registered full. A moment later, she eased the Chevy down the deserted alley and headed out.

She was near the prison within a matter of minutes, the road coming up so quickly she almost missed it. She found a place to pull the car into the underbrush and parked, the engine ticking loudly in the dark. Sprinting into the jungle past the giant rubber tree she'd used for a mental marker, Meredith made her way back to the spot where she'd left Haden, her footsteps fast but silent.

He was right where she'd left him.

Shaking him into consciousness, she half dragged, half walked him back to the car. The trip that followed was a blur.

Pulling into the driveway of the safe house three hours later, she climbed wearily from the car to reverse the process, tugging and pushing until she had Haden safely inside.

CHAPTER FIVE

WITHOUT BOTHERING to undress him, Meredith propped Haden up in the shower in the downstairs bath and turned on the water full blast. When she came back ten minutes later, he was in the same position. She turned off the faucet and he opened his eyes.

She responded to their pull despite her best intentions to remain aloof. What the hell had she gotten herself into? She forced herself to play the role she'd already decided would work the best—the hurt but resolved former lover who wasn't sure how to proceed.

"We need to talk," she said.

"I think you said everything you needed to when you pulled out your knife."

"I explained that."

"No," he said. "You lied. Lying is not an explanation."

"What more do you want?"

"How about the truth?" he suggested. "Something tells me you must be as interested in hearing it as I am otherwise we wouldn't be having this discussion, would we? Two monkeys would be fighting over my guts back in the jungle instead, and you'd be in Miami having a cool one by the pool."

She couldn't argue with his logic.

"Who sent you?" he asked softly. "Was it Reynolds? If it was, there are some holes in the briefing he gave you…but I guess you've realized that now, haven't you?"

The mention of Reynolds's name made her stiffen. "You're nuts," she said bluntly. "What would make you think he's involved in this?"

He smiled crookedly. "I'm right, aren't I?"

"Why don't you just explain why you were in that prison to begin with? From what I've heard, you have to piss off some pretty bad folks to end up there. What'd you do?"

He put his hands on either side of his legs and pushed himself to his knees. Using the ledge of the shower for extra help, he made it to his feet. She expected him to slide back down but he didn't.

"I'll show you mine," he said after a second's rest. "If you show me yours. But first I have to get my head screwed on a little better."

His reply wasn't what she expected and her guard went up even higher. "What do you mean?" she asked suspiciously.

"I need clean clothes and bandages, maybe even

an aspirin if it's not too much to ask. I want something to eat. I'd like to rest. It's a simple trade, Meredith. No tricks. Help me out and I'll tell you what you want to know."

She didn't trust him but the confidence she'd had in her mission was slipping, too. She hesitated for another second, then said, "I'll go see what I can find. Don't go anywhere."

Shutting the bathroom door behind her, she climbed the stairs to one of the bedrooms on the third floor. When she'd arrived, she'd seen some jeans and shirts hanging in one of the closets. Thinking they might fit him, she grabbed one of each then came back down and dropped them on the floor outside the door, the sound of running water filling the silence of the house once more.

He emerged half an hour later, the jeans riding low on his hips, an unbuttoned shirt clinging to shoulders still damp from his shower. Looking up from the stove where she was scrambling him a plate of eggs, Meredith stared as he shuffled into the kitchen.

With the grime gone and some of the swelling down, he almost looked human, but she had to hold back a groan at the damage that remained. The cut by his temple still looked awful.

He raised his eyes to hers. "Can you stitch me up?"

She swallowed. "It's not one of my favorite things

but I can probably handle it. There are some supplies upstairs—I checked."

"Good. I didn't want to do it myself."

Neither of them mentioned a doctor because both of them knew better.

He sat down at the table. She put the eggs and some toast on a plate then set it before him, along with a mug of coffee.

He started to dig in, then stopped, suspicion darkening his features.

"You already pointed out the obvious," she said. "Besides, if I wanted you dead, it wouldn't be by poisoning." To make him feel better, she picked out a piece of the egg and ate it herself.

Staring at her with a measured glance, he nodded once, then he began to eat. The rest of the food was gone before she could take her own seat. She arched an eyebrow. "Do you want some more?"

"That'll hold me for a while," he answered. "Aren't you going to have something?"

She shook her head and wrapped her fingers around the mug of instant coffee she'd made for herself. "I'm not hungry," she said. "I'd rather hear your story."

He pushed back from the table and stretched his legs out before him. "There's not much to tell," he said. "I think you know more about this situation than I do."

"I doubt that," she answered, "but first things

first." She leaned her elbows on the table and sent her eyes over his beat-up face. "Who did this to you?"

"I don't know," he said. "The introductions were neglected. I came home and someone was waiting for me behind the door. That's all I got. When I woke up, I was at the prison."

"Have you pissed off Fidel Menchez?"

"Who?"

She could tell by the look in his eyes he was being genuine. She repeated the name. "He was your host," she explained. "The prison is his."

"I've never heard of the man. But the bad guys come and go in this part of the world."

"Maybe you upset one of his buddies. I've been told he does favors. Maybe you were one of them."

"I have no idea. They weren't happy with me, whoever they were."

"Were you hiding something? They did a pretty good job of tearing up your house, too."

His eyes widened. "You went there? That wasn't a smart thing to do."

"I thought you were dead." She ignored his criticism, her voice going quiet. "There was blood everywhere."

"Yeah, well, that's not too much of a surprise. It's a miracle I have any left." He gripped his mug, took a sip, then spoke. "How'd you find me?"

She held up a hand and silenced him. "Not so fast.

We're not finished with my questions yet. I'm not answering any of yours until I get more information myself."

"Then you may have to beat it out of me just like they did," he said. "Because I don't know any more."

"You knew enough to mention Dean Reynolds's name," she said with speculation. "Why did you bring him up?"

His expression shifted. If she hadn't known him so well, she wouldn't have noticed the change.

"You're here," he said. "Reynolds was always your buddy. I thought he might have sent you to finish me off."

"Why would Reynolds want you dead?"

"You tell me."

"He wouldn't sanction one of his own agents." She waved a hand airily dismissing the notion. "That doesn't make any sense, does it?"

"It makes none at all, as far as I'm concerned," Haden agreed. "But I can't argue with the facts. You didn't come down here to see the sights and that wasn't a butter knife you pulled out back there at the prison. I'm wondering why you missed, though. That's not like the Meredith I know. Are your reflexes slowing?"

His words stung. She stood, her emotions in a turmoil as she crossed the kitchen to stare out the window above the sink. In the reflections painted on the glass, she could see Haden's face. He looked drawn and weary and once again she wondered what in the hell she'd gotten herself into.

"What do you know about Brad Prescott?" she asked quietly.

His expression reflected no surprise. "I met him at a party a few weeks ago. We talked. He disappeared two days later."

She turned and stared at him. "That's all?"

"No." He stared back. "There's more. But I'm not sharing it with you."

"C'mon, Haden—"

"C'mon, nothing. I don't trust you any more than you trust me," he said. "And on top of that, I sure as hell don't trust Dean Reynolds...which is where, I suspect, all this is leading." He pushed himself up from the table and approached her, his body so close to hers they were almost—but not quite—touching. His eyes drew her to him. "Reynolds is in the middle of something down here, Meredith. Something really bad."

She held her breath. "That's funny," she confessed after a second. "He said the very same thing about you."

"Somehow I'm not surprised by that. Reynolds has a way of turning things around to suit himself."

"He doesn't need to turn anything around," she argued. "He's the director. You're an agent. He didn't get behind that desk by making mistakes."

"That's true," Haden conceded. "But I haven't survived this long by making too many of them myself." He added softly, "You haven't made very many of them, either. But this could be a big one if you listen to him. Maybe you need to think about that."

"What are you telling me, Haden?"

He looked out the window behind her. After a moment, his expression deepened and he seemed to come to a decision.

He leaned over, turned on the faucet behind her, then trapped her, his hands on the kitchen counter at either side of her, his voice a hoarse whisper above the running water. "If you're setting me up for your boss, you'll come to regret that decision, Meredith. I'll hunt you down like a dog and when I find you, it won't be pretty."

Meredith held her breath at his threat, then she shook her head. "That's not what's going on here."

His eyes bored into hers. "You better be telling me the truth."

"I am."

He stared at her a little longer, then something in her expression seemed to convince him.

"Reynolds's name has been linked with Rodrigue Vega's," he said. "Vega's a local kingpin with ties up north. He's into drugs, smuggling, you name it. When I talked to Brad Prescott before he was kidnapped, he'd had too much to drink. He thought I was a nobody at the Embassy and he told me he had a little business venture going with Reynolds. I'd say somebody got upset when they learned that I checked out Prescott's hotel room later. They probably wanted me out of the way until they could decide what to do with me. Wouldn't you agree?"

Meredith's dark eyes flared but before she could speak, Haden covered her lips with his finger and continued, his mouth against her ear once again. "The word on the street is that Vega's men grabbed Prescott. Make the connection, Meredith. Draw the lines. Prescott to Reynolds. Reynolds to Vega. Vega to Prescott. I'd say we have a circle, and inside that circle we have three people." He drew back slightly and looked at her. "You and I aren't in that circle, babe. What does that tell you?"

"It doesn't tell me a damn thing." Her voice was sharp but she kept it low. She wanted her words disguised by the sound of the running water just as much as he had. "If this is your idea of trading information, I'm not buying."

"You're *not* buying anything," he shot back. "I'm *giving* you the truth for free." He dropped his gaze to her mouth then lifted it to her eyes. "What are you giving me?"

"Let's go to the bathroom," she said. "I think it's time we tend to those stitches."

THEY LEFT THE KITCHEN and headed back down the hall. The bathroom was still steamy and the air held the scent of soap and shampoo. Haden found himself remembering all the showers he and Meredith had taken together. After sex, before sex, during sex…their soap-slicked bodies had come together in ways he hadn't even thought were possible. He shook the memory from his head and trailed her to the sink. From a built-in medicine chest to her right, Meredith proceeded to remove enough supplies to tend to a small army, including a bottle of antibiotics, two of which she gave him right away. When she had her equipment lined up, she nodded toward the leather-covered vanity chair behind him.

"You probably want to sit down for this," she said ominously.

He followed her advice, then watched as she flipped on the radio occupying the windowsill behind her. She wanted their voices covered just as he had back in the kitchen. She picked up a cotton ball and doused it in alcohol, then moved between his knees. To take his mind off what was coming, he placed his hands on her hips as if steadying himself. Beneath his fingers, her body felt as firm as ever.

The alcohol was cold where it touched his freshly scraped skin, but the sensation it left behind was painful and hot. He winced and focused on the necklace she wore to distract himself some more. It looked like platinum and it held a single, tiny diamond. He'd never figured her for a diamond and platinum kind of woman but then again, he'd always felt as if he'd never actually known her that well, despite their relationship.

She continued to dab at him, her lips inches from his ear when she spoke. "What do you think Prescott, Dean and Rodrigue Vega are involved in? If they even are," she added quickly.

"I don't know," he said. "But it's got to be something pretty big if Dean sent you down here."

She pulled back as her eyes flashed to his. "I never said that he did."

"You don't have to," Haden said. "I know he did. We can leave it at that."

She got a clean cotton ball then turned back to him. "If we're going to speculate, then why don't you go out on a limb and ask me what you think they're doing, too?"

"I'm not sure," he said slowly. "But the more I think about it, the more I keep going back to the screw-up in Libya. Do you remember that deal?"

Her forehead wrinkled. "Are you talking about the assassination attempt on Sudi Benifar?"

He nodded. The elderly Arab had been one of the more democratic rulers in the Middle East and a staunch ally of the United States. On the Saudi peninsula to meet secretly with the president, he'd barely escaped with his life when his black Mercedes had been blown into a thousand pieces two seconds after he'd climbed out of it. His assassination would have thrown that part of the world into utter chaos but he'd survived.

"I remember it," she said, "but that happened years ago. What could that have to do with this situation now?"

"We never figured out who was behind the attempt on Benifar's life," he reminded her. "No one was supposed to know he was even in that country."

"That was investigated," she said warily.

"Yes, it was. And nothing was ever resolved."

"They were standing in line to take a crack at Benifar. It could have been anyone."

"That's true," he agreed again. "But Al Balsair wanted him worse than anyone else. Abu Zair is the head of that organization and he's hated Benifar forever. We didn't know it back then. At that point, we thought Zair belonged to us. He was the point man for State during the investigation."

She pulled in a sharp breath, her reaction one of shock. "Are you saying Zair and Dean Reynolds may be working together—"

He started shaking his head before she could finish. "First we stick to our deal. You promised me some answers, too. Give me some answers of my own before this goes any further."

"You'll get them when I'm ready."

"No." He grabbed her arm and stilled her movements, his grip as tight as his voice, his threat hanging in the air between them. "I'll get them now. I want to know how you knew where to find me. If I were a suspicious man, I might wonder if you had something to do with me ending up in that prison in the first place."

"I told you. Fidel Menchez—"

"That's the who. I'm asking about the how."

Her jaw tightened but she answered. "You're not the only one with contacts. It wasn't that hard to find you."

"Then why didn't you expect me when you saw me? I know I looked bad but you didn't recognize me."

"I thought I was going to find Brad Prescott." She shook off his fingers and began to thread the needle she'd pulled from the first aid kit. "I thought you were dead, but I was wrong so it doesn't matter now, does it?"

"Just tell me this—what were you doing hunting for Prescott in the first place?"

"You don't need to know that."

"I disagree." He stopped her one more time. "Because someone threw me in that shit hole and after I find out who it was, I intend to even the score. If Prescott had something to do with that, I want to know."

"And if he didn't?"

"Then you can pass that on to your buddy, Reynolds, in case he needs to be prepared instead."

"I will," she said calmly. "Now close your eyes and sit real still."

MEREDITH STEPPED BACK and admired her handi-work. The stitches looked good, especially considering how badly her hands had been shaking after Haden had revealed what he had.

Turning back to the first aid kit, she took out the bottle of painkillers and shook out two, handing them over to him. He washed them down with a bottle of water, then went to the front bedroom. Five minutes after his head hit the pillow, he was sleeping so deeply, he almost looked dead.

Meredith watched him from the doorway. She'd only meant to peek in and make sure he was resting, but once she'd realized he was out, her feet had refused to move. She stared at him and wondered about everything he'd told her.

Reynolds had said Haden had gone bad.

Now Haden was blaming Reynolds.

The story Haden had laid out wasn't as detailed as Reynolds's had been, but she and Haden worked within a twisted world—specifics could be manufactured. As strange as it sounded, the truth was often murky and that's how you recognized it. Just the hint of this being linked to the Libyan situation, however, had taken away her breath. Was he playing her? Her mind ran over the possibilities but all that came to her were more questions, the most pressing one being the most obvious one: If Reynolds had been lying to her, then how had Haden ended up in prison?

She cursed as she stared at the sleeping man. She had to have more answers but she knew Haden well enough to know she wasn't going to get them unless she gave him more.

Was the risk worth taking?

Haden murmured in his sleep and threw out an arm to the empty side of the bed as if feeling for someone who should be beside him.

She wondered if he was dreaming about the woman he'd been kissing in the photograph Reynolds had shown her. Haden had said nothing about her, but then again, he'd had no reason. It hadn't been *her* photograph that Meredith had found in the rubble, though. She'd found a picture of herself. So what did that mean?

She tightened her jaw, then turned away and headed back down the hall. She didn't need to worry about who occupied Haden's dreams.

She only needed to decide if he was lying to her.

If he was, he wouldn't be having many more dreams, regardless of who was in them.

THE SMELL OF FOOD woke him up and for a moment, Haden wasn't sure where he was. He remembered almost instantly but the lapse disturbed him. Sliding his legs to the side of the bed, he felt his stiffened joints complain but all in all, he felt better than he had since the night he'd been dragged from his house. He crossed the bedroom to the mirror on the opposite wall, glancing out the window he passed in the process. It was dark outside. He'd slept the entire day.

His face remained swollen but he definitely looked more like himself, the bandage Meredith had applied to his cheek an improvement just on its own. He touched it gingerly. She'd done a good job sewing him up. He'd seen the small careful stitches before she'd covered them and he'd remembered she'd told him once she'd wanted to be a doctor when she'd been a kid.

He wished she'd pursued that dream.

Watching her as she'd listened to what he'd said, he'd wondered how much she was buying. Her ties with Dean Reynolds went deep. Convincing her the old man might be involved with something shady would take a lot. Meredith understood the power of truth, though, and if he could say enough to make her wonder, he'd have her on his side. For awhile, at least.

He made his way through the house and found the kitchen once more. Meredith was standing by the stove, stirring something in a pot. She turned the instant his foot cleared the threshold. He'd caught her unaware once. It wouldn't happen again.

"You're awake." Her eyes traveled over his face, cataloging the injuries. "You look a little better."

"Thanks to you."

"Consider it payback for rescuing me at the prison."

"You always did like to keep score," he said.

She shot him a look he ignored, then he helped her carry the plates and glasses to the table. She'd made *albondingas,* she explained, because the ingredients had been handy. The soup was thick and surprisingly good.

"You never cooked for me before," he said as she sat down.

"Don't get excited," she retorted. "I may never do it again."

She was clearly on edge and he didn't blame her. Twice she got up and left the table without a word, her footsteps quiet as she checked on something. A door? A window? He didn't know and he didn't really care. All he wanted to do was get some food down and then resume their conversation.

He got his wish as soon as they finished eating.

"Let's go outside," she said. "There's a patio out back."

She'd left the television on inside, but she didn't trust it to cover their conversation. They escaped the sound of the blaring set and let the humid darkness envelop them, Haden slipping into one of the lounge chairs on the cobbled stones, Meredith taking the one right beside it.

"I want to hear more about your theory," she said. "What makes you think there's a link here to the Middle East?"

He shook his head. "No way. It's your turn now. You answer some of my questions first."

She'd expected him to refuse. She answered with obvious reluctance but still tried to stall. "Like what?"

"Like did Reynolds send you?"

"He contacted me. All we talked about was Prescott, though. I was supposed to find him. When I got here, I decided to go by your house first." Her gaze went past him then came back. "I knew something had happened but I didn't expect to see you at that prison."

"You never do anything spontaneous, Meredith. Save the crap for someone who doesn't know you."

"It's the truth!" she protested.

He leaned closer and dropped his voice. "You came down here for a reason and I'm beginning to think that reason was to kill me. You didn't expect to see me at that prison, but you were sure fast to take advantage of the situation. You didn't follow through later, because I surprised you when I mentioned

Reynolds. Tell me what's going on, Meredith, or we stop this game right here."

A stubborn look came over her face, one he'd seen before.

"If Reynolds is behind this, you better be damn sure you have some evidence of what he's telling you," he argued. "He's a slippery bastard. You could end up holding the bag on this one, Meredith, and I don't think that's something you want."

Her eyes rounded in surprise. She clearly hadn't considered the possibility of a setup, which told him just how much she continued to trust Dean Reynolds.

"He gave me proof," she argued, as if reading his mind.

"Proof about what?"

She waited a second, then said, "He told me you had turned and that you needed to be removed. He called you a traitor to your country."

"A trai—" Haden broke off, his anger rising. "What the hell is he talking about?"

"He showed me photographs," she said. "Pictures of you with Brad Prescott and others. Two of the men looked like operatives from the Middle East. I thought I recognized them, but now I'm not as sure as I was then." She paused, then seemed to plunge ahead. "There was one of you and a woman, too. He said she was your contact with Al Balsair."

"Al Balsair?" For one stunned moment he simply stared at her, their previous conversation rising up to haunt them.

"It fits a little too well, doesn't it?"

"Why didn't you tell me this earlier?"

"I had to think about it," she said. "Then I realized something. Photographs can be faked…but prisons are for real. Someone wanted you out of the way and they made damn sure it happened."

He stood up and came to her side, his fingers reaching out to tuck a strand of hair behind her ear with an absentminded motion, his fingers brushing over the edge of it. "Reynolds is smart," he said. "He didn't make things too complicated. He accused me of what he's doing and left it at that."

She came to her feet, her hand going to her throat. *"What?"*

"The rumor mill's been grinding for weeks down here. I'd heard that someone was smuggling people into the United States. When Prescott mentioned his involvement with Reynolds I got even more worried."

"But what made you think of Al Balsair?"

"Don't you remember who headed the investigation after Benifar survived?"

She kept her eyes on his but shook her head.

"Reynolds was in charge of it, Meredith. His only task was to find out who wanted the Saudi dead, but his report was never conclusive."

She frowned and Haden kept talking.

"Reynold figured out then that Zair was behind the bombing, but Zair paid him to keep it quiet and that's what Reynolds did. Now they're working together again—smuggling terrorists into the States. And Vega's helping. He has a lot of contacts in the Middle Eastern community here—we have a huge population of Arabs for a Latin American country. Prescott's involved somehow, too. I searched his hotel room after he disappeared but I didn't find anything."

"I know you did. Dean told me your prints were all over the room. He offered to let me talk to the police—"

"Prints! I didn't leave any prints there, Meredith! C'mon, do you think I'd be that stupid—"

"Then how—"

"They were already following me," he said slowly. "They knew I went to the hotel and that I was figuring it all out and that's why they snatched me."

"Why send me?"

He felt his jaw tighten. "I don't know. Maybe Reynolds just wanted to tidy up the place after he realized I'd talked to Prescott. Maybe he planned that little riot that broke out because he thinks we both know too much. Maybe we were both supposed to be hit after you got there. Two birds with one stone and all that…"

"But what about Prescott?" she asked in a worried voice. "What's happened to him?"

"If they know he let Reynolds's name slip, then he probably told someone else, too. That would be reason enough for them to get rid of him."

"Do you think he's dead?"

"I don't know," Haden answered. "But if he isn't, I'd say he will be shortly. Maybe we should talk to him, before he meets that fate."

CHAPTER SIX

THEY WENT TO SLEEP shortly after that, but unable to rest, Meredith got out of bed early the following morning and sat down beside the phone, an even greater sense of urgency than before forming inside her. Haden's prediction about Prescott was lying heavily on her mind. If anyone could unravel this mess, it might be the engineer from Redman. He *was* the only sure link she had between Haden and Reynolds. She picked up the telephone and made two calls. The first to arrange for another safe house and the second to Barrisito.

The fixer's voice was hoarse with anger over someone disturbing his sleep before he realized who was calling. "You're alive," he said with relief. "We knew the car was gone, but we weren't sure you had gotten to it. Things are *muy loco* in Huehue right now. The prison riot left many dead."

"I know," she said. "I saw the bodies. Is your brother all right?"

Barrisito made a sound of disgust. "He's fine but

I should have left him there. I know things did not go as you had planned."

"That's true but the car was where it should have been and it got me back to the city."

"Did you get your man out?"

"I did," she answered. "But I'm still looking for the other one. Any word?"

"I'm working on that. My brother might know more. I'll ask him when I get him home."

She thought of Haden's theory about the riot. "How did the situation get so out of control? How did the fire happen?"

"I don't know," Barrisito sighed. "My brother said that before he could start the fight you had told him to initiate, the fire, it broke out."

"Was it an accident or did someone start it?"

"He couldn't tell. Things went too crazy too fast."

She let his words hang in the air, knowing all the while that "things" didn't just happen. Someone had to have started that fire deliberately. Could Haden be right? Had Dean been involved with it? No one knew she'd been going to the prison except Barrisito and his brother. She trusted Barrisito but everyone had a price.

They said their goodbyes and she hung up the phone. She started to punch out another number but her fingers stilled when she heard Haden coming down the stairs. Watching him cross the hallway to enter the room where she sat, she understood her inability to sleep the previous night. The wall that had separated them hadn't been thick enough. She'd known he was on the other side of it. She could have sworn she'd been able to hear him breathing and she'd wanted to lay her head against his chest and feel it as well.

She didn't like the emotion but there was no stopping it. She still had feelings for Haden and she'd been a fool not to acknowledge them—to herself if no one else—when Dean had called her. Haden padded toward her.

He stopped at her side, his open shirt flapping. "You're up early."

She turned on the radio sitting on the desk to cover their voices. "I wanted to call my contact." Her voice was more abrupt than it needed to be but every time Haden came close, she started having thoughts she didn't want to have. The inability to control her mind was maddening.

She told him what Barrisito had said about the riot.

"How good is your man?" Haden asked. "Is it possible—"

She'd just asked herself that very question, but Meredith rose to the defense of Barrisito and his brother, interrupting Haden before he could finish. "He's good. I've used him for years. I don't believe he had anything to do with what happened." And she didn't, she decided quickly. "You get what you pay for in Guatemala and he isn't cheap. He knows better than to cross me, anyway."

Haden sent her a speculative look. She ignored it and continued. "We've got better things to worry about anyway. I thought about what you said and I think you're right about Prescott. We've got to locate him." She paused. "And we've got to move. We can't risk staying here another night."

"I thought about that myself. It's too risky. If Reynolds knows you're here—"

"He doesn't know where I'm staying," she assured Haden. "I never told Dean. Then again, he didn't know I was going to the prison, either. It'd be a good idea to find a new place anyway."

"You didn't trust him from the very beginning."

"I wouldn't say that—"

"I would." Haden stepped to her chair then bent down, his eyes on the same level as hers as he interrupted her. "You knew better all along than to believe him."

"You think so?"

"I *know* so."

"Why is that?"

"You have good instincts." He trailed a finger down her arm, leaving a tingle in its wake. "You knew I couldn't be all bad or we wouldn't have had what we did. It was too hot—"

"No, no…" She stopped him abruptly. "Let's get something straight about that right now, Haden. What happened back then was a mistake. It shouldn't have occurred. You were my boss, for God's sake."

"So what?"

"'So what?'" she repeated. "So everything! Screwing the man you work for isn't a good idea and it never has been. I should have had my head examined."

"It wasn't something we could control."

"That's baloney," she said, "and you know it. We didn't *want* to control it or we could have."

"Maybe… And maybe not." His eyes glistened in the morning sun that poured through the window beside her. "Either way, you can't deny it was good."

"I can deny anything I want to," she said stiffly. "But it doesn't matter one way or the other now. It's over. Past history. Done and finished."

"I don't think so…."

"Then think again—"

His voice toughened. "We wouldn't be having this conversation if you believed otherwise so don't pull that shit with me. I'd be dead if you didn't care. Just admit it now and we'll get all this behind us."

She pulled in a deep breath. He was right. If they got everything out in the open maybe it'd go away. Maybe she'd be able to sleep. Maybe she'd get her head on straight.

Ghosts ran when you looked at them during the day.

"Let's just say you have a point, for the sake of this argument," she said. "Let's just say what we had was good and that I did care."

He nodded.

"Things are different now than they were back then. We've moved on," she said. "You've got someone else and I'm in a different place, too. We need to concentrate on what's ahead without our past hanging between us. It's only going to get in the way."

His fingers stilled on her arm. "What do you mean I have someone else?"

"I saw the photos," she said. "You and the woman. Dean showed them to me."

"What are you talking about?"

"He had pictures," she said. "Remember? I told you about them last night. One of them showed you two kissing. She was very pretty—dark hair, dark features." Meredith hesitated. "Dean told me she was your contact with Al Balsair but it was pretty obvious you two had something more going on."

Haden jerked to attention, his expression angry. "I've been with one woman down here and that was Desiree Lopez. She *is* one of my contacts and we *were* close, but it's been over for months."

Meredith stared at him, an unexpected relief hitting her at his revelation. She pushed her reaction away. "It doesn't matter," she said quickly. "I don't care—"

"Well, I do," he said.

She analyzed his obvious irritation. Haden had clearly planned on using their former relationship to his advantage but with another woman in the picture, he knew that plan was foiled. Meredith's resentment flared.

What he said next surprised her, proving he had a deeper understanding of the situation than she had thought.

"If Reynolds had a photograph of the two of us, then he's been planning this a long time, Meredith. I haven't seen Desiree in at least six months, probably more. Whatever Dean Reynolds has going, it must be something big."

MEREDITH SEEMED to digest his words but she dismissed his point a second afterward. "Maybe it is," she said, "but if we can't stay alive, we can't figure out what Reynolds is doing one way or the other. I've found us another place and all I care about is getting us there. We aren't safe here."

Haden started to challenge her but he let the matter drop. She was right. They'd been reckless to even stay the previous night. They needed to move on.

Thirty minutes later, that's exactly what they did.

Meredith left first. He watched her walk briskly down the sidewalk heading south until she went around the corner. Ten minutes after that, he headed out the opposite direction, his step even quicker. The risk of someone recognizing him was higher than he would have liked. The place they were heading to was on the other side of town, in a barrio few expats knew existed. They'd be in less danger there, at least in that respect.

Before she'd slipped out the front door, Meredith had told him the address and given him further instructions. "Come directly to the house," she'd said, "and keep a sharp eye out. If anything feels funny, call me and I'll find us somewhere else to go."

He'd nodded with a serious expression and repeated the address she'd given him. "I'll be there," he promised.

Reaching the end of the street, he hailed a cab and was gone two minutes later.

The address he gave the driver wasn't the one Meredith had given him.

They headed instead for Zona 9, an upscale part of Guate that contained a mixture of older homes and villas. Some of the city's more distinguished families lived in the area and the house Haden's cab finally stopped before was one of the larger and more expensive ones. He paid the driver but told him to wait.

He didn't want to be on the street any longer than he had to.

Looking both ways, he strode up the sidewalk and rang the bell. A uniformed maid appeared within seconds, her face a blank as she stared at him through the gate. "*¿Sí?*"

She didn't recognize him and he didn't recognize her, but Haden wasn't surprised. Desiree went through help almost as quickly as she did men.

"Is *la señorita* home?" he asked. "I'm a friend. I need to talk to her."

"She's home," the woman confirmed "But she's sleeping. No visitors." She turned and started back toward the front door.

"*Momentito, por favor...*"

Something in his voice stopped her, and she turned and came back. "Wake her up," Haden suggested. "She'll be glad that you did."

The maid looked down, then her hand flashed through the iron bars to take the pesos he held out.

"Wait out here," she said, releasing the latch to the gate. "I'll check."

He sat on a bench beneath a wooden arbor and closed his eyes, the scent of gardenias filling the air around him. Desiree Lopez lived in a different world than most of the Guatemalans Haden had come to know during his stay. The daughter of a rich industrialist, she'd had everything she'd ever wanted, in-

cluding an education from Harvard. Her friends
came from the wealthiest echelons of Latin American society and she knew their secrets. Dismayed
by the political chaos of her country, she'd wanted
to help stop the corruption that had sucked the very
life out of it for so long, but she'd had no idea how
to do so. Then she'd met Haden at a Christmas party
and they'd hit it off. The cooperation that had
followed started out professional but it had quickly
turned into something more. She'd broken it off
three months later, telling Haden she didn't believe
in long-term relationships. He'd been relieved. He
couldn't keep up with her.

After twenty minutes of sitting in the garden,
Haden was ready to give up. Then the front door
opened. Desiree stood on the threshold in a filmy
white robe. The sunlight shifting through the windows behind her created some interesting shadows.
He lifted his eyes to her face and read the shock that
filled it over his appearance.

"Jack Haden," she said slowly. "What happened
to you?"

He stood up and crossed the patio. "I ran into a
door."

She didn't get the joke, but he didn't care. "It
doesn't matter," he said when she frowned. "Have
you got five minutes? I need to talk to you."

She smiled. "For you, Jack, I always have the

time. Come inside." She stepped back but not too far. He had to brush past her to enter. Her eyes met his when their bodies connected but the spark he'd once felt wasn't there. He realized why when Meredith's face came into his mind.

"I missed you," Desiree said softly.

"I've missed you, too," he said. "But I'm here for a reason and that isn't it."

She shut the door behind her, something in his attitude obviously reaching her. "Let's go in my office."

They entered a room just off the main entry. It'd been her father's study. The tile floor was covered with a fine silk rug and the walls were paneled in rare Guatemalan canarywood, the variegated pattern striking in the morning light. Two sets of French doors opened to the courtyard. Visitors could come and go without entering the house itself. She turned to Haden, the expensive furnishings a part of her life for so long they didn't even register with her. "What's wrong?"

"I've gotten into a little situation," he said. "I wanted to let you know since it might involve you."

She arched one perfect eyebrow. "This sounds serious."

"It could be."

"Tell me more."

"I will but first I have to ask a favor. Do you still have that snub-nosed .38?"

She tilted her head. "*Sí*... I have it."

"I need it," he said.

She seemed to weigh his request; then she opened the top drawer in the desk at her side and reached inside. When her hand reappeared, the black pistol lay in her palm, along with a roll of cash. She'd known what he was going to ask for next. Muttering his thanks, he checked them both before tucking the pistol into his waistband and the money in his pocket.

"Someone from here is smuggling a very special kind of contraband into the States. Have you heard about this?"

Her expression seemed to shift, the high cheekbones and full lips tightening slightly. She knew everything that went on in the city, but she was judicious when it came to sharing information. She always held something back. Sometimes it was information and sometimes it was herself. This had bothered him at first, until he came to understand. He did the same thing only in a different way. It was a protective measure, a way of keeping back an ace.

This time he couldn't allow her the luxury.

"Do you know anything about this?" he pushed. "I have to hear it if you do."

"I may have heard something," she hedged. "I do know the people who are involved in things like this can be *muy peligroso*. Rodrigue Vega is one of them, no?"

"He could be," Haden said. "Do you know any of the others?"

She shrugged. "There could be a man from the States. Someone high up."

"Do you know his name?"

"No. Do you?"

He didn't answer.

"If you do, I would be very careful. Anyone who does business with Vega is not a person to be ignored. There are rumors about how he dissolves partnerships that no longer profit him and lawyers are *not* involved. I've heard he has a compound close to Belize. Many of his associates go there to visit…and never return."

"Do you know where this compound is?"

Her face closed again and he wasn't surprised. "No. I don't know where it is located. I don't want to know."

He stared at her—she was holding her ace more securely than usual, and this time she wasn't turning it loose.

"I understand," he said finally. "But you *will* want to know this—photographs were taken of you and me and shown to a friend of mine. She was told you were a representative of Al Balsair. You know the organization?"

Desiree didn't have to answer. Her widened eyes did it for her.

He continued. "I want you to be careful. If you

think Vega is bad, this could be worse. It may come to nothing but you never know for sure."

"What should I do?"

"Sit still," he said. "Act as if you don't even know. But if anything unusual happens, I want you to call and leave a message." He handed her a card. The number he'd scrawled on it belonged to a cell phone with voice mail. "Do you understand?"

She looked up from the card. "Are you in trouble, Jack Haden?"

"Nothing I can't handle," he said. "But thanks for asking."

Neither of them had sat. She came to where he stood and touched the bandage on his face with gentle fingers, her perfume coming with her. "Will I see you again?"

Surprised she even cared, Haden ran a thumb down her cheek, then kissed her, the action leaving him cold and unmoved. "I don't think so," he said quietly. "This is probably goodbye."

He headed for the double doors, but her voice stopped him as he reached for the elegant gold handles.

"Is she worth it?" she asked.

He paused and looked over his shoulder. "Who?"

"The woman you're involved with," she asked. "You're obviously in love. Is she worth your life?"

Haden smiled at her perception. "She's a real killer," he said. "Only time will tell."

THE HOUSE WAS SMALLER and darker, the neighbors so close she could smell their lunch. Meredith looked around and nodded in satisfaction. For what they needed now, it was perfect. She paid off the man who'd found her the place and locked the door behind him, glancing at her watch. She had ten minutes before Haden was supposed to arrive and she had to make every one of them count.

The first thing she did was grab the cell phone she'd had the man pick up for her. There had been no time to charge the unit but she could use it while it was plugged in.

She dialed the number from memory and prayed she was doing the right thing.

The woman who answered spoke in clipped tones. "Advanced Scientific Laboratories. How may I direct your call?"

"Extension 346," Meredith replied.

Canned music played for so long Meredith began to despair. Then Steven Blacker answered. "Yeah?"

She didn't identify herself. "I need some help and I need it fast."

"What's new?" The twenty-something lab rat was a poster boy for Tommy Hilfiger. Looking at him, you'd never know he spent hours up to his elbows in blood and gore every day but he did. And with great results. The ASL facilities were top-notch and

Meredith had used them for years. "You're always in a hurry." He didn't say her name, either.

"Yeah, well, this time I'm in a bigger hurry and you have to keep it quiet. I especially don't want you saying anything about this to anyone else there in the lab. Or anywhere else."

The kid liked to brag to his friends about the "spook" work he did and Meredith played him relentlessly. She did so now even more than usual. "This is a blacker than black ops. Do you understand what I'm telling you?"

"You got it," he said, his voice perking in interest. "No one hears a word from me. What's up?"

"I sent in some butts the day before yesterday. Have you gotten them?"

She could hear the frown in his voice. "Cigarette or cigar?"

"Cigarettes. They were Payasos from Guatemala."

Papers shuffled and then he spoke. "I don't have anything like that around here. Are you sure they've have enough time to arrive?"

She cursed softly. "I sent them overnight…but there's probably a different definition of that service down here than there is in the States."

"We've been really swamped," he said. "Let me go to the mail room and check. Maybe the package just hasn't made it up here."

"That'd be great." She waited a beat, choosing her

words carefully. Dean didn't know where she had her lab work done but there was no such thing as being too careful. "I'd rather they didn't go through the usual channels. Is there any way you could skip the log-in procedures this time?"

"Not a problem."

"Good. I wasn't sure what I wanted done with them when I shipped them to you, but they've become a little more important since then. Do the usual stuff, but run them through ITD, too."

This time, his tone went guarded. "I need a special code to access the International Terrorist Database. Do you have it?"

"Of course I don't," she said. "Why would I be calling you and telling you to do it if I had that?"

He laughed. "I gotcha. I'll contact my friend Jesse in Homeland Security. It might cost you something."

"Can he keep his mouth shut?"

"Of course." His voice went defensive.

"All right, then. Put it on my tab," she said. "Just do it fast and—"

"—and keep it quiet. Can I call you back at this number?"

"No," she said. "It'll be dead in a few hours. I'll call you."

She punched the end key then sat back and frowned. The package should have arrived by now.

What had happened to the cigarette butts she'd found in Haden's house? Had they somehow been intercepted? The idea sounded far-fetched to Meredith but not as much so as it would have earlier.

Just like it'd never occurred to her that Dean might be setting her up. When Haden had voiced the idea last night she'd been shocked but after sleeping on it, she'd realized he could be right. Her father had always worried about that very thing.

"Plausible deniability," he'd pounded into her head. "You have to have plausible deniability. It's your insurance, Meredith. Make sure you always have it no matter how good the job sounds."

She'd ignored the advice, just like she'd ignored a few other key issues. All because of Haden.

The thought sent her eyes to her watch and with shock, she saw an hour had passed since she'd left the other safe house.

Where in the hell was Haden?

CHAPTER SEVEN

MEREDITH GOT HER ANSWER an hour later when
Haden slipped in the back door without a sound. The
time between her question and his arrival was filled
with anxiety and she didn't appreciate him putting
it there. She had enough to worry about already.

"Where have you been?" She pointed angrily to
her watch. "It shouldn't have taken you more than
fifteen minutes to get here. You've been gone almost
two hours!"

"I had a stop to make," he said. "What are you,
my mother?"

Her face heated. "I was worried. I thought—"

"That I'd gotten away from you?"

His comment hit home. That was exactly what
she'd assumed but she kept it to herself. "I thought
something might have happened to you," she said.
"I guess I shouldn't have worried, though, should I?
You're obviously just fine." She stared a little closer
at a red smudge on his cheek, then felt her anger go
up a notch. "Real fine…"

He frowned, then looked at himself in the glass that fronted the oven, his thumb going up to the smear of lipstick. "I went to see Desiree," he said, stating the obvious.

"You shouldn't have done that. Every minute you're out on the streets means another minute someone could have spotted you." She strode to the window and stared past the burglar bars that covered the glass. Unlike the previous safe house, this one fronted the road. She turned back to him, her thoughts in a jumble. "What were you doing, Haden? Why'd you go see that woman?"

"It wasn't a tryst, if that's what you're worried about."

She felt her jaw flex. "I couldn't care less," she said. "I thought I made myself clear about that this morning."

"I assumed you'd reconsidered," he said.

"You assumed wrong." She started to continue, but realized he was distracting her on purpose. "What *were* you doing there, Haden?"

He opened the refrigerator and pulled out an apple and a hunk of cheese. Both looked as if they'd been there quite a while. "I wanted to warn Desiree," he said quietly. "If your buddy Reynolds has photos of her, that's not a good sign."

"You told her what was happening?" she asked in an incredulous voice.

He bit into the apple and looked at her. "I gave her a warning. I owe her that much, Meredith, and probably more. I had to go. It was the only decent thing to do."

Emotions rolled inside Meredith, relief, confusion and anger all mixing up together. The fact that he cared about the woman made Meredith remember all over again what kind of man he really was, but he'd put them both in jeopardy by going to her house. It was vintage Haden and it left her in her usual dilemma, part of her admiring what he'd done, the rest of her angry.

"I understand," she said after a bit.

"No, you don't." As if finally noticing how bad it was, he tossed the apple into the trash can in the corner. "But that's okay, too."

MEREDITH NODDED ONCE, then left the room, her back stiff with an anger Haden didn't understand. Was she upset because she thought he'd escaped or anxious because he'd gone to see Desiree? Neither answer felt right so he decided to just ignore the whole episode.

He thought instead about what Desiree had told him. If Rodrigue Vega had a compound in the north, it was probably close to Tikal. There wasn't much in that direction except for the ruins and Flores, a smallish town forty miles south that rested entirely on an island in the middle of Lake Peten Itza. Vega's villa would probably be easy to find, the miserably humid town was a tourist trap and little else.

Haden leaned against the kitchen counter and thought through the situation. If Vega and Reynolds *were* smuggling people into the States as Reynolds had accused Haden of doing, then they were probably sneaking them over the border via Texas and that meant going through Mexico. Having a home close to the Mexican border would make meetings with the terrorists that much simpler. They could avoid Guate and possible detection by flying directly into Flores. The place had a decent airport. From there, it'd be an easy thing to get up to Tikal or wherever Vega's villa was and make their plans. They might even be using the man's compound as a way station of sorts.

It'd be equally easy to make people disappear permanently from there. Tikal was a spooky part of the country, the ruins and the jungle coming together to create a dark, dense prison where escape wasn't an option. It wasn't too hard to hide bodies in a place where the vegetation grew so quickly. Throwing a few terrorists into the mix almost seemed logical in a twisted sort of way.

It wasn't a part of Guatemala Haden liked. Then again, he was beginning not to like quite a bit of it. Maybe the time had come for him to go somewhere else.

If he survived.

He pushed away from the kitchen counter and took a quick tour of the house. Meredith had chosen well. The place was small and therefore easy to secure, the windows few and narrow. He found her in one of the tiny bedrooms upstairs, a laptop computer open before her as she sat cross-legged on one of the beds. She glanced up from the keyboard as he paused in the doorway. She appeared preoccupied with whatever she was doing and he decided that was a good sign—whatever had set her off had been replaced by a new concern.

"I'm trying to get some information on Prescott," she said. "But something isn't right."

"What do you mean?"

"There's no record of him entering Guatemala," she replied. "No commercial flight info, no visa info, nothing. Officially, he's not here."

"Well, unofficially, I saw him."

"What day was he snatched?"

He told her and her fingers flew over the keys. A few seconds after she quit typing, she shook her head. "Nothing in the police records. That's even stranger—"

Haden came to the edge of the bed and sat down on the mattress. "The national police probably handled the kidnapping since he's American."

"That's not what Dean said—" She stopped herself abruptly.

"You've already started," he said. "You might as well finish."

"He told me the Guatemalan City police had been notified by someone at the Marriott. He said they had checked out the disappearance." She looked back at the computer. "But there's no record of that here."

"Does that surprise you?" he asked.

"After all we've discussed, I guess it shouldn't, but still…" The keys clicked beneath her fingers again, and she frowned as she read the screen. "There's no record of anything in the national police files, either."

Impressed by her skills, Haden jutted a chin toward her computer. "Are you that good a hacker? I would think the government records might be a bit tighter than that, even in Guatemala."

"I'm talking to someone in the U.S.," she explained. "And yes, he is that good." She leaned back against the headboard and stared at Haden. "But I don't think he can find a dead man and without a ransom demand, I'm afraid we may already be too late," she said. "In fact, if Vega *did* grab Prescott, I can't think of why Vega wouldn't kill him as soon as he could."

"That may be the case," Haden replied. "But I think he'd want to get as much information as possible out of Prescott before he did that." He waited a beat, then spoke again. "There's only one way we're going to find out the truth and that's to find Vega and ask."

"And just how are we going do accomplish that?"

"I know where he lives," Haden said smugly. "Desiree told me."

SHE'D FOUND his proximity distracting, but Haden's announcement had Meredith focusing quickly. "How on earth would she know what was going on?"

"Desiree stays connected—to everything and everyone. She told me that Rodrigue Vega has a house close to Tikal. Prescott certainly wasn't in the prison they put me in. So if—and that's a big if—Prescott is still alive, Vega might be holding him in Tikal. That's where his compound is."

"That makes sense."

"If I were Vega, I'd want to know who else Prescott spilled Reynolds's name to," Haden agreed. "But who knows? Maybe Vega has other plans for him. Prescott had just come in from the States so it's possible—"

The random pieces Meredith had been studying suddenly seemed to fall into place. She put her hand on Haden's arm, her voice excited. "That's *exactly* what Prescott's doing and Reynolds practically told me so."

Haden looked at her with a puzzled expression.

"I asked Reynolds why he was bothering with the

disappearance of someone like Brad Prescott and he told me the employees of Prescott's company— Redman Communications—had been flagged because they had people going in and out of Guatemala so frequently. He said that was the link between you and Prescott. He thought Prescott was carrying money or goods for you."

"He's carrying something all right," Haden said slowly. "But not for me."

Meredith nodded, her excitement over figuring out Prescott's role fading when she understood the implication. "He's the intermediary between Reynolds and Vega."

"But something went wrong and Vega's men grabbed him instead."

They looked at each other, each understanding at the same time. "He was going to run with the cash?" Meredith suggested.

"Probably so," Haden agreed. "Which means he wasn't just arrogant, he was stupid, too."

"He's a goner."

"Yes."

"But we still have to try to find him. What's the best way to get to Tikal? Can we fly?"

"There's a fairly large airport in Flores. We could fly in and rent a car. It's about forty miles north."

"No," she said slowly. "That's not the way to do

this. Reynolds would have people checking the airports. We can't risk it."

"We can drive. A new road went in a few years ago. It connects Flores with Guatemala City, but it goes straight through the middle of Peten, which is pretty dangerous territory." He paused then sighed heavily. "It'll take forever but we'll probably get there in one piece if we take the bus."

"Perfect. I'll get the tickets in the morning." She spoke but her mind remained on Reynolds, her thoughts about his involvement coalescing just as her realization about Prescott had. How could she have been so wrong about the man who'd helped her for so long? He'd been her mentor for years. Had he been using her all this time? Which of her hits had been legit and which had been his doing? The question left her nauseous.

"You just can't believe your buddy would do something like this, can you?" Haden's voice broke into her thoughts. "You can't believe Reynolds is involved."

"I don't *want* to believe it," she confessed, "but I don't have a choice in the matter. You've said enough to make me want to question what's happened so far, and I can't just look the other way, no matter how badly I'd like to do so. No one is above the law."

"That sounds real good, Meredith, but I guess it's a philosophy that doesn't apply to you, huh? You *are* the exception, aren't you?"

She felt her face go warm but his question wasn't unexpected. She'd been waiting for him to bring back the subject of her work. However, explaining the Operatives to Haden was not something she could do. Not now. Not ever.

"Am I right?" he pressed.

She unwound her legs and dropped them to the side of the bed. "I wouldn't say that," she hedged.

"Then what would you say?"

She looked at him directly. "I wouldn't say that," she repeated.

Their stares came together in the hush of the bedroom then something changed and his gaze became pointed and sharp. "Why not?"

She waited a second before starting to rise. As she did so, he reached out to grab her forearm, but he moved too slow, his reflexes obviously still affected by the beating he'd had. She escaped his touch and walked to the doorway where his voice stopped her.

"When are you going to tell me?"

She turned slowly, her mouth going dry. "Tell you what?"

"When are you going to tell me why you do what you do?" he said. "You're going to have to give me a reason sooner or later, you know. You kill people for a living, Meredith. I want to know why. We can't keep ignoring the elephant in the living room."

"I have no idea what you're talking about, Haden.

I think you must have suffered a head injury during your beating. You need to lie down and rest for a while. You're not thinking straight."

She left the room without another word and the rest of the evening passed in the same kind of silent vacuum. It was still early when she escaped the tiny living room and went upstairs to go to bed but once again, her night was restless, the image of Haden sleeping on the other side of her bedroom wall keeping her awake for far too long.

She woke early and left the house for the bus station before he got up. It was only a few blocks away, and she wanted to check the schedule to Tikal.

Despite their proximity to the station, however, she hailed a cab and had him drive her around the neighborhood for ten minutes. She wanted to make sure no one was following her. Finally she had the driver head to the bus station. He did as she requested and asked no questions; he was happy to have the money and knew better than to open his mouth.

"Wait here," she said when they got there. "I'll be right back."

He was sitting in the same spot when she came out a few minutes later. She had him drop her four blocks from the house and walked quickly through the morning haze. Stopping at the corner *tienda*, she picked up some fruit and milk, but even as she shopped her questions continued to haunt her, the answers elusive.

If Reynolds was involved, why had he sent her to Guatemala? Did he think she was so stupid, she wouldn't figure out the truth?

What *was* the truth?

She rounded the last corner and started down the sidewalk, her eyes studying the area ahead of her for anything unusual. Three kids were playing kickball in the middle of the dusty street, a dog racing beside them trying to get the ball. Two women, their arms crossed over bulging stomachs, watched from the opposite side. Four doors down from where they were staying, a table had been set up in the filtered shade of several large jacarandas. Two old men sat at the table, smoking and sharing cups of *café con leche* and a plate of mango slices.

Meredith continued down the broken concrete walkway until she reached the house and disappeared inside.

CHAPTER EIGHT

HADEN WAS WAITING at the kitchen table when Meredith walked in. She dropped her purse and a plastic grocery sack on the table before him and pushed a strand of hair back. "I got the tickets to Flores," she said. "We leave tomorrow morning at eleven. There wasn't anything sooner."

"That's good," he said. "No problems?"

"Not that I saw. I had the cab drive me around a bit and leave me at the corner but I didn't see anything unusual."

"I'm glad we're getting the hell out of here." Haden stood, the restlessness he'd felt on waking that morning intensifying with every hour. He didn't feel safe in the city but he didn't tell Meredith that. "I don't think I could stay here for too long."

She looked at him with a frown. "Why not?"

He moved to the window that looked out over the street, his mood turning pensive. "It reminds me too much of where I grew up." His words had been an excuse but as they came out, he realized he was telling her the truth. Tilting his head toward the kids running around outside, he spoke. "That could be me and my brothers, thirty years ago. Playing in the street with sticks and a stolen ball. Living in the same house as my grandparents, all of us crammed in it like a bunch of rats."

"Where was this?"

"In San Antonio. We were so poor I didn't have a piece of clothing that hadn't been someone else's first until I left college and joined the Marines. Growing up without money is hell."

They'd never had this kind of conversation before, and it made Haden wonder how well they really knew each other. When they'd been together before, they'd shared no real closeness, he thought with a jolt. Sex, yes, intimacy, no.

"How did you manage college then?" Her curiosity seemed genuine. "If your family didn't have any money—"

"I went to the University of Texas in El Paso on an athletic scholarship," he said. "Football. After each game, I worked as a janitor and helped clean the stadium. During the week, I waited tables every night." He rubbed his shoulder and grimaced. "God, how did I do it?"

She crossed the room to stand beside him. "You were younger and no one had just beat you half to death," she said quietly. "That makes a difference."

She reached up and took his chin between her fingers to turn his head. "I need to change that bandage tomorrow."

For a moment, they looked at each other in the morning sun, then Meredith seemed to pull back, the momentary closeness dissolving in the light. Who was he trying to fool? She might have asked the questions, but she wasn't interested in him. She'd told him so.

They spent the rest of the day running their contacts and fishing for information. Each came up empty-handed, Desiree's tip the only thing they had to go on. By nightfall, the edges of Haden's nerves were frayed and raw. His temple throbbed and his stitches were beginning to itch. He thought about pulling them out, then decided to leave them until morning. She wouldn't like him messing with her work, but he couldn't stand them any longer. The scar was going to be there one way or another so what did it matter?

They scrounged a meal from the contents of the pantry. When they finished eating, Haden turned on the circa 1980 television set in the tiny living room to catch the news and Meredith disappeared upstairs. Above the sound of the announcer's voice, he could hear her talking on her cell phone.

He went upstairs a little before midnight. A light still shone under her door and he paused before it, his hand raised to knock. He stopped himself at the last minute, his knuckles a breath away from the wood. What was the point? Dropping his hand to his side, he turned and went to his room.

"JUST A MINUTE, Blackie," Interrupting the conversation she'd been having with the tech in D.C., Meredith put her hand over the cell phone and cocked her head toward her bedroom door. She listened for a second, then went back to the conversation, the sound she thought she'd heard obviously imaginary. She was edgy and unsettled, and listening for ghosts was something she did when she felt that way. The feeling had started when she'd spoken earlier with Cipri. His brother had finally returned, repeating his story that the prison riot had started without his help. Since Meredith didn't believe in coincidences, this news bothered her. Now, after getting Steven Blacker's report, she was even more nervous.

"Are you absolutely sure?" she asked again. "We can't have any mistakes on this one."

"I don't make mistakes," he said, his voice huffy. "You know that better than anyone."

She rubbed her forehead and stared out the window beside the bed. She'd cracked it open and the smoky smell of the city had crept inside. "I know," she said, "And I'm sorry if I insulted you but this just sounds so weird."

"It may sound that way," he said, "but I can't argue with the results. Your package came in right after you called and I started to work on it immediately. I double-checked—no, triple-checked—everything."

"It's just so unexpected."

"The database doesn't lie. Every employee of a federal contractor is now required to have his fingerprint registered with the government, whether he's working on a project for them or not. The time is coming when we'll want DNA samples, too. It's a brave new world since 9/11."

Her mouth felt fuzzy, her brain even more so. "And his name is Brad Prescott? You're sure?"

"Brad Prescott, 907 Steamboat Springs, Houston, Texas. Social Security number, 879 87 7665, Texas driver's license number 075896. Height five feet eleven—"

"Okay, okay…I get it."

"When we didn't get a hit in the terrorist database, I just thought 'what the heck' and I ran through our other db's. This isn't a mistake."

"I understand."

The silence built up over the line between them, then she said, "You haven't told anyone else this, have you?"

"Of course not." His aggravation with her questions seemed to grow. "No one even knows I was working on this except Jesse. He had to help when I needed into the ITD but he knows how important this stuff is."

"Make sure he keeps it all to himself, Steven. Some bad things are happening down here and I don't want you or your friend to get hurt."

Her warning seemed to pull him up short.

"Is that a...um, possibility?"

"I don't know for sure, but it could be. The people who may be involved in this situation are high up and if they're doing what it looks like they're doing, then they're going to be very anxious to keep their part in this quiet. The best thing for you and your friend to do is lie low and keep busy. If anyone asks you about it, act like you don't know a thing. Don't even let on we've spoken." She pulled in her bottom lip. "You're at the pay phone, right?"

"Yes."

"Good." She thought for a minute. "Did you sample all the butts I sent?"

"Absolutely. They were all the same."

"All right," she said finally. "I appreciate everything you did. This info really helps. And Steven?"

"Yeah?"

"Stay safe, okay?"

"That's the plan."

Meredith punched the end button and cut off the call. Stripping off her clothes, she took a quick shower then crawled in bed, her mind spinning.

What were cigarettes with Brad Prescott's finger-prints on them doing at Haden's house? The man had supposedly been kidnapped two days *before* Haden had been beaten and dragged to Menchez's prison. Had Prescott escaped? If so, why come back and beat up Haden? Could the butts have been there before? Haden had said nothing about Prescott coming to his house, but if Reynolds had told her the truth and Haden had lied, it was entirely possible the engineer would have visited Haden at his villa. Where else would they have conducted their business?

Her doubts bloomed again.

Was Haden lying?

Troubled and confused, Meredith finally fell asleep but her eyes popped open a few hours later.

Something wasn't right.

The cheap digital clock beside the bed glowed with green light, the numbers reading 3:00 a.m. She slid her hand under the pillow to her left. Her fingers wrapped around the hilt of her knife and she pulled it out slowly, the grip warming in her palm. Listening closely, she heard nothing more. Then five minutes later, whatever had woken her sounded again.

Tap…tap…tap…

She tensed and edged out of the bed, her bare feet cold against the polished wood floor. A second later she pressed herself flat against the wall, her fingers twisting the doorknob so slowly the movement was undetectable. She pulled it open slowly.

She looked through the crack that opened up between the trim and door. She saw nothing but darkness. Widening the gap, she tilted her head to glance into the hallway.

At the other end of the corridor a gleam caught her eye and she froze. A heartbeat later, she realized it was Haden. He was standing at the threshold of his room, as well, a small, snub-nosed pistol held stiffly in one hand. He'd heard what she'd heard, but what was it?

He raised a finger to his lips, tilted his head toward the stairs, then pointed to himself. She nodded and circled her hand. He would check out the downstairs; she would do the top floor.

They passed each other in the hall, Haden going one way, Meredith the other. Her knife held loosely, she opened the first door she came to. It was the third bedroom and she eased inside it without a sound. She checked under the bed and then the closet. Seeing nothing, she turned to the small narrow windows on either side of the headboard. They were locked securely, their screens intact. The house might have been humble, but the owners of even the most modest homes in Guate tried to keep their screens secure. Malaria wasn't something anyone wanted to encounter.

She turned to the bathroom that adjoined the room but it was empty as well, the window set above the tub not only locked but painted shut. A sledge-hammer would have been needed to open it.

She started down the hallway then stopped outside Haden's room. He'd obviously been inside it when the noise had sounded but she couldn't leave the upstairs without securing it as well. She walked inside and checked it just as she had the one across the hall, looking under, around and behind everything she could. Nothing seemed wrong. Her eyes landed for one quick second on the tangled sheets, the blanket half off, the pillows askew. Haden had always been a restless sleeper—it didn't appear that had changed.

She left the room and headed for the stairs, her feet sliding soundlessly across the floor. Gripping her knife at her side, she made her way down the steps, one at a time, her eyes scanning the downstairs as it opened up before her.

The central room was empty, the front door locked. The only place left was the kitchen. It faced the front hallway with an arched doorway separating it from the rest of the house. She crossed the living room then slipped around the opening.

Haden was sitting on the floor, petting a white kitten. Meredith paused on the threshold and he looked up.

"I found our intruder," he said ruefully. "There's a pet door off the pantry. We must have heard him batting at it. When I came in here he shot out from under the table and scared the heck out of me."

Meredith flicked her knife shut and slid it into the pocket of her shorts, realizing as she did so, what she had on. Her sleeping ensemble, loose boxers and a camisole, wasn't her most flattering but judging from the look on Haden's face it didn't really matter. The appreciation that shone in his eyes was something she hadn't seen in a while. It made her feel sexy and appealing and suddenly self-conscious.

She turned abruptly. "I'm going back to bed—"

"Meredith, wait…"

She looked over her shoulder with a questioning glance. He'd stood. The cat was winding figure eights about his legs and meowing.

"I heard you on your cell phone before I went to sleep. Did your contact here find out anything else about the riot?"

His question explained the noise she thought she'd heard. He'd obviously paused outside her door when she'd been talking to Cipri. She considered telling him about the butts and Prescott's fingerprints, then decided to keep the information to herself.

"The guy who helped insisted he didn't see who started the fire," she said, stalling. "That's all."

The cat wrapped his paws around Haden's ankle and nipped at his toes.

"You better feed that guy," she said before Haden could ask anything more, "or he's gonna start gnawing on you."

He nodded and turned to the cabinets behind him, opening them until he found a can of tuna. He dumped it on a plate then set it down on the floor. The animal inhaled the food then looked up to beg for more.

"Do you still have Chuy?" Meredith asked without thinking. She'd never been a cat person but Haden's giant tiger-striped calico had been an exception. A real queen, she'd been an expert at subtlety and intrigue and had made Meredith like her despite her best intentions not to.

"I gave her to my nephew," he said. "I didn't want to move her down here and she'd lost interest in me, anyway. She was bored and needed someone new." He looked up from the kitten. "You know how women are," he said with a smile. "They're always needing a fresh challenge."

Meredith leaned against the doorjamb, her need to return to bed forgotten. Or maybe pushed aside. "Not that you want to generalize, right?"

He crossed the room without answering and she became aware of what he was wearing, too. Or more specifically what he wasn't wearing. He had on a pair of boxers and nothing else. His chest was a road map of bruises and cuts and his back looked even worse.

"I'm just stating the obvious." He stopped an inch away. "Is that what happened to you?" he asked. "Did you need a new challenge, too?"

Meredith tensed. "As I recall, *you* were the one who threw me out."

"I'm not talking about our breakup," he said softly. "I'm talking about the path your career took. Did you need something different to do? Is that why you went the way you did?"

She started to turn but he stopped her, his fingers flashing out too fast to escape. "Tell me the truth, Meredith. You're going to have to sooner or later."

"Then let's make it later," she said.

He shook his head. "Now."

"You'll never understand," she said softly, her eyes meeting his. "And it wouldn't matter if you did because I can't explain it."

"Can't or won't?"

"Why do you even care?" she asked, desperate to change the subject. "We would have never made it, anyway, Haden, and you know it. We weren't meant to be together."

"You don't know that," he said. "Not for certain."

"Are you crazy?" she asked. "We're too different. We would have ended up in jail…or the nuthouse."

He dropped his fingers and shook his head, his blue eyes unreadable. "You've got it backward," he said.

"What do you mean?"

"We're too *alike*," he said. "And it *would* have worked if you'd wanted it to."

With that, he pushed past her and walked up the stairs. Too stunned to reply, Meredith stayed where she was, her eyes falling to the cat that was now washing its face. When it finished, it went to the pet door and pushed its way out, the *tap…tap…tap…* of the door sounding loud in the kitchen's silence. Shaking her head, she turned and followed Haden's path up the stairs, crawling back into her bed, the sheets now cold.

When the sun came up, she was still wondering what he'd meant.

THEY MADE THEIR WAY to the bus station the next morning by separate routes, Meredith leaving first. She'd looked at Haden before going out the back, her eyes glinting in the morning sun, her fingers gripping her backpack. "The bus leaves at eleven. Are you going to be there?"

He'd stroked a finger down her jaw and she'd tightened her lips into a very straight line. "I'll be there," he'd reassured her. "Why wouldn't I be?"

She hadn't answered him. She'd simply turned and gone upstairs. Ten minutes later, he'd departed the house.

His mind stayed behind, however, and concentrated on how she'd looked when she'd walked into the kitchen last night. For a few small seconds, he'd been unable to speak. The camisole and shorts had taken him back in time, and he'd remembered the hours they'd spent together in bed, touching each other and whispering silly secrets. He shouldn't have said what he did, but he hadn't been able to stop himself. They *were* alike. In the middle of the previous night, which was when he did all his heavy thinking, he'd come to that conclusion after giving it a lot of thought. Both of them came from restless backgrounds, both of them loved their country, and both of them knew their own limits. Very few people understood that last thing, he'd come to realize, but Meredith did.

And so did he.

They were both loners who didn't fit in. Loners who needed each other because no one else would understand.

The contradiction didn't bother Haden, but he focused on what that really meant. He couldn't have killed for money so why would Meredith?

He let the question sink in deeper then pushed it aside. He had to concentrate on the here and now or it wouldn't matter what Meredith had been doing. They'd both be dead.

Walking into the busy bus terminal, he glanced

around. The tile floor echoed every sound and there were plenty of them to repeat, from crying children to crying adults to crying vendors. Everyone had something to say and the cacophony was as over-whelming as the grime and poverty. The bus system in Guatemala was the transportation of the poor and anyone who could tried to find another way to travel. The trip to Flores would take fifteen hours and Haden wasn't looking forward to it.

But running into some federales at the airport wasn't something he wanted, either.

He adjusted the cap he'd put on before leaving the house, then hefted the bag on his shoulder and waded into the crowded station, making his way through the throngs with a constant *Perdóname, perdone...* Finding the nearest waiting area to the bus they would be taking, he spotted Meredith almost imme-diately out of the corner of one eye. He continued forward without acknowledging her, taking one of the empty chairs a row over from where she sat.

They waited twenty minutes, neither of them looking at the other. Finally the number of their bus was called. Meredith stood first and started toward the exit but Haden remained behind. He waited another ten minutes, then stood. A moment later a commotion broke out near the front of the terminal. His pulse accelerated when he looked across the mass of travelers and saw what was going on.

Three federal police were standing by the front door, their hands on their guns, their dark uniforms and shiny hats sending a quiver over everyone in the building. They immediately engaged the security guard in a heated discussion and the guard was clearly losing. Even as Haden watched, two of them got impatient with the conversation and broke away to stride into the center of the terminal, their eyes flicking over the crowd as they walked. They were looking for someone.

Haden didn't wait to see what happened next.

Pushing his way past the gawkers, he pulled his cap down farther and walked toward the gate in what felt like slow motion, his mouth going dry. He made it to the threshold, the smoky morning haze throwing a blanket of humidity over him as soon as he stepped outside. Looking neither right nor left, he continued to where the bus waited and handed his ticket to the collector, who gave him a dirty look for waiting so long. Ignoring the petty expression, Haden climbed onboard and made his way to the empty seat next to Meredith. They didn't speak until the bus reached the outskirts of Guatemala City.

CHAPTER NINE

"WHO WERE THEY?" Meredith broke the silence first, glancing at him as she spoke.

"*Los Federales*," he answered under his breath. "I don't know them but I recognized the uniforms. And the arrogance. It's standard issue, along with the gun."

"What were they doing?"

"Looking for someone."

She tensed. "You?"

"I didn't stick around to find out."

She watched the changing landscape out the window. The last of the industrial buildings and small manufacturing plants were in the distance when she spoke again. "This is getting complicated."

"It wasn't before?"

"I talked to my lab guy last night." She'd decided on her way to the station that she had to tell Haden about the cigarette butts. She wasn't sure what had made up her mind but she suspected the decision had something to do with how he'd looked at her last night. His eyes had held a warmth that couldn't be faked. It'd disturbed her greatly.

"What did he say?"

She turned away from the window. "The butts I picked up at your villa had Prescott's fingerprints on them."

Shock filled his expression as two small vertical lines formed between his eyebrows. "Brad Prescott? Are you sure?"

"My guy doesn't make mistakes." She repeated Steven Blacker's proclamation because he was correct. He'd never gotten anything wrong.

"That doesn't make sense. Prescott was kidnapped two days before I got beat up. How could that be?"

Meredith let the silence grow, then said, "He escaped? He wasn't kidnapped at all? He has a twin brother? You tell me." She narrowed her gaze. "Maybe he left them there the last time the two of you got together to plan your next deal?"

"There weren't any *deals*." His eyes turned angry. "I only met the man one time and that was at the French Embassy."

Reynolds's voice sounded in Meredith's head. "Dean made it sound like you two were friends."

"I'm sure he did. That sounds exactly like something he would do." His face filled with disgust. "He always starts out with the truth but then he twists it until it suits him. It's one of his favorite tricks."

She stared at him because she couldn't look away. "Why do you hate him so much?"

"I hate him because he's a user. He makes people do what he wants, then he pushes them out of the way when he doesn't need them anymore." He paused. "One of these days I'm afraid you might be the one he pushes."

"I'm a big girl." Her words were tough but the idea of Haden worrying about her touched her in an unexpected way. "You do what you have to," she said. "Especially in this business."

"'*This business...*' Are you referring to *your* business or *my* business? They're two different animals, you know."

"You know what I mean."

"No, I don't. Why don't you explain it to me?"

She ignored his question. "Was Brad Prescott the man who hurt you?"

"I was too busy defending myself to look. But he didn't strike me as the kind of guy who could handle a lot of blood, if you know what I mean."

"Why leave that kind of proof?"

"He wouldn't have thought about it," Haden said, dismissing the idea. "He didn't strike me as the sharpest blade in the drawer."

"Could someone have planted it?"

"To what end?"

"Who knows? Maybe to throw us off?"

"No one even knew you were coming here—" He broke off and their gazes clashed.

"Except for Reynolds," she finished quietly.

He nodded.

Meredith fell silent after that. The rest of the trip was marked by a series of stops, one after another. Vendors came onboard as soon as the bus's brakes quit squealing, and tried to sell them everything from T-shirts to blankets. Most were hawking cold drinks that weren't cold and stale nuts or crackers. Haden gave in after a few hours and bought them some of each, after which they were able to simply hold up the cans so the salesmen would leave them alone.

By the time they finally pulled into Flores, they were exhausted and grimy. But safe.

Haden found a cab and Meredith gave the driver the address Barrisito had given her. He had a cousin who rented out rooms. Another girl had a friend, who had a friend, who knew someone who *might* be able to help them locate Vega's house. They would be contacted, Barrisito had said mysteriously. The cab pulled away from the bus station, its tires thumping over the brick streets noisily. The house where they were staying was in Santa Elena, off-island, but Flores itself was in the center of Lake Peten Itza. Meredith stared across the water as they drove past, the round isle looking unchanged since the last time she'd been there. The night air that slipped inside the cab as they traveled was hot and sticky.

Meredith snuck a quick glance in Haden's direction. He'd been quiet ever since she'd told him about the cigarette, but she didn't know if that was because he was thinking or if he was tired. The bus ride had been brutal and he wasn't a hundred percent by any means. She started to ask him how he felt, then she kept the question to herself, something holding her back.

The car pulled to a stop in front of a modest two-story villa, a spill of blossoms from a nearby bougainvillea gleaming darkly beside the brightly lit front porch.

Meredith rang the bell and the door was opened a moment later. The woman who stood on the threshold wore a friendly smile, her long dark hair framing a face that had been beautiful when she was younger but would now be described as striking. *"¿Sí?"*

"We have reservations." Meredith used one of Barrisito's many names. "We're friends of Sr. Gomez."

"Oh, yes, yes… Please come in. I've been waiting for you." She stepped aside and motioned for them to enter the house, her eyes flicking over Haden's battered face for only the briefest of seconds. "I am Sonia Delgato, Gomez's cousin. He called and told me he was sending me some business."

Meredith wondered what kind of cousin, then dismissed the thought. "We were relieved you had a room on such short notice."

The tiled hallway was cool and dark. "We had some unexpected guests, but I saved you something upstairs. I'm afraid it has twin beds, though." She sent Haden a quick look. "Is that all right?"

"That's fine," Meredith replied before he could speak. "We just need a place to sleep that's quiet and private."

"I understand," the woman murmured. "Follow me, *por favor...*"

After a quick tour of the downstairs, she led them upstairs to a corner room. Before entering the bedroom, Meredith looked down the hall and pointed to a doorway at the end.

"Where does that go?"

"Those are the back stairs," Delgato answered politely. "They go out to the patio but the maids use them, as well."

Meredith nodded with satisfaction then walked past her to go into the bedroom. It was clean but spartan, two narrow beds pushed against the walls with a table in between.

"The *baño* is through there." Delgato gestured to a door beside one of the windows. "I serve breakfast at nine. *Café* and *pan dulce,* unless you'd like something else."

"That will be fine." Haden spoke for the first time. "We appreciate your hospitality."

She smiled at him, her eyes flashing. "Is the hour too early? Perhaps you'd like to sleep later?"

"Nine is perfect," Meredith answered firmly. "We'll see you then."

Delgato sent a sympathetic shrug in Haden's direction then closed the door behind her.

MEREDITH SHOWERED FIRST. By the time Haden came back from investigating the downstairs more thoroughly, she had tucked herself into the bed nearest the door and was asleep, the lamps off. At first he thought she was pretending, but when he looked closer, he realized she really was out. He studied her in the darkness and tried to analyze the feelings that had been bombarding him since he'd seen her cross the prison yard and come toward him.

What was it about her that drew him so close then pushed him away? No answer came to him.

He took a quick shower, the stall fragrant with Meredith's shampoo, then climbed in the other bed and closed his eyes, but his mind refused to shut down. He began to analyze the information she'd given him about Brad Prescott. Could he have been the man behind Haden's door?

Haden frowned in the darkness and tried to remember more details, but he'd been attacked so quickly, nothing had registered except pain. He vaguely recalled the crash of furniture and his attempts to fight back. They'd been futile from the beginning, his attackers too fierce to overcome.

The thought brought him up short. Attackers? There *had* been more than one, he realized with sudden surprise but until this very moment, he'd forgotten that. He concentrated harder but nothing more came to him. Half an hour later he was still gazing at the ceiling.

With a sigh, he turned over and stared through the shadows at Meredith's outline under the sheets. It wasn't easy to go to sleep with an assassin resting three feet away.

Not when he'd rather be in *her* bed than his.

MEREDITH GOT UP EARLY and ran four miles, her excess nervousness forcing her to release the energy or explode. When she came back, Haden was still asleep and the sight of him in the other bed undid all the good her run had just done.

She was dressed and eating breakfast in the dining room when he finally showed up. Sonia greeted him at the door with a smile and fresh fruit. She handed him the plate then turned and picked up a coffee pot from the sideboard. "Would you like some *café, señor?* I have bread coming out of the oven in five minutes."

Meredith watched; Delgato's smile was as warm as the coffee she was offering.

Haden responded with a grin of his own. "Thank you, Sonia, that would be great."

The exchange grated on Meredith's nerves and the fact that it did bothered her even more. She was acting like some kind of hormonal teenager, for God's sake, one minute attracted to Haden, the next distrustful and cautious. She'd faked being asleep after he'd come out of the bathroom last night, but she'd felt his eyes on her in the dark. She'd wanted to ask him what he was thinking and why he was doing what he was doing. She'd wanted to sit beside him and talk for hours like they had before. But she couldn't. And that made her mad as well.

When he came to the table and sat, she spoke brusquely. "Another of Sr. Gomez's 'cousins' found me this morning while I was running."

Haden tilted his head.

"She's lucky to be alive." Stabbing a slice of pineapple with her fork, Meredith recounted the episode. "She grabbed me just as I went around a corner and I reacted before I realized what was going on."

"How many holes did you put in the poor girl?"

Meredith felt her mouth go tight. "She gave me an address," she said. "I'm leaving in five minutes. I'll be back by eleven. I assume you'll be here?"

"I'm going with you."

"No, you're not."

"I want to hear what's said."

"I'll tell you when I return."

They stared at each other from across the table, then after a second, Haden leaned closer. "What's wrong with you this morning?"

"I keep my network confidential," she said. "People won't talk if I show up with an entourage."

"I'm one person," he said calmly. "And whoever he is, your man would talk to a stadium full of people, if you pay him enough. Don't treat me like I don't know what's happening."

"I don't know this guy," she argued. "If you show up, it could spook him—"

Haden took her chin in his fingers, his touch soft, his voice low. "What are you doing, Meredith? Are you trying to make me not trust you? If you are, it's working."

She felt relief that he'd misunderstood her emotions but it didn't last long. "I'm *trying* to do this the right way." She moved her chin away from his hand. "We need some information if we're going to find Vega's compound. Your girlfriend was a little lacking in the details. I'm doing my best to fill in her blanks."

"She's not my girlfriend," he said, his gaze steady

and level. "And we're damn lucky she gave us what she did. Otherwise we'd be up the creek."

"All right," she said. "I'll take you with me but I do all the talking."

THEY SET OUT ten minutes later and grabbed the first taxi they saw. Meredith gave the driver the address, then turned to Haden, the tension inside the cab so thick he was surprised it wasn't visible. She was on edge but he had no idea what was behind her nervousness. It wasn't the meeting, though, that was for sure. Meredith didn't get rattled by things like that.

Why did women have to be so complicated?

"We have to cross the causeway," she said, "and go into Flores itself."

"Who are we meeting? Did you get a name?"

She shook her head. "The girl told me where to go then she ran off."

He turned to the passing scenery. The sky seemed to reflect Meredith's mood, ominous-looking clouds churning overhead. As they crossed a long, narrow bridge, the smell of rain drifted in through the open window. Once on the island, the cobblestone streets were congested, everyone honking horns as if the noise would help. The buildings on either side were all painted, their faded stucco walls showing the city's connection to the nearby Caribbean, the soft pinks and greens and yellows reminiscent of St.

Thomas and the other islands just to the east. He took in their condition with a grunt of surprise—the lower floors of a few, and the foundations of more, were flooded, the water lapping against their walls. Canoes and kayaks, along with some less identifiable modes of water transportation, were secured in the waterlogged streets along with the cars and trucks.

"The island is sinking." Seeing his reaction, Meredith pointed to a chipped stucco structure that looked unoccupied. "There used to be a street on the other side of that building, but you can't use it anymore. The water is rising all along the perimeter of the island and flooding the lower-lying homes. They've actually had to abandon some of the buildings."

"You've been here before?"

"Once," she said. "I had to meet someone here. About a job."

Haden started to ask, then stopped. She wouldn't have told him more, regardless.

When it became obvious they weren't going to move anytime soon, they got out of the car and made their way on foot. It was faster and cooler, and within ten minutes, they were standing before a modest iron gate. Meredith rang the bell that was set in the wall. Fat raindrops were beginning to fall when a little boy, five or six, shot from the front door and ran down the sidewalk to greet them. The boiling clouds began to rumble.

Haden's Spanish was good but he couldn't follow the kid's excited jabbers. Seeing his puzzled expression, Meredith translated as the boy unlocked the gate. "His *abuela* is home," she said. "She's been expecting us."

Haden looked at Meredith in surprise. "His grandmother?"

She shrugged. "The woman didn't tell me who we would be talking to. All she said was there was someone who 'might' be able to help us."

They followed the child into the house just as the rain began in earnest. The hall was dim and gloomy because of the weather, but Haden suspected the lack of light was deliberate as they walked farther into the home. Everything from the furniture and rugs to the floor itself was dark and old. Even the walls contributed to the feeling of murkiness. They were incredibly thick, the windows set back in the stucco at least two feet, velvet drapes hanging on either side. He felt as if he were entering a cave.

It seemed as if they walked for a long time, the structure much larger than it appeared from the outside. Finally they stopped at the doorway of a sitting room. Haden's eyes were still trying to adjust when a querulous voice could be heard from the depths of a chair set in one corner.

"Who's there?"

The child answered and Haden caught a few words this time, the main one being *gringos*. Haden squinted, the form of a woman in a chair emerging from the shadows as they stepped farther into the room. She was dressed in black and wore her hair long, a silver plait hanging to one side of her face. She stared at them sightlessly.

Meredith shot Haden a helpless glance and her expression said it all. Their contact was old, housebound and blind. What kind of information could she possibly have for them?

Meredith approached the woman in the chair and spoke softly, introducing herself and Haden. "We were told you could help us find someone who lives near here," she said.

"Who told you that?"

"A friend of mine from Guatemala City."

"Why do you need to find this person?"

"He's broken the law. We're here to stop him."

The old lady didn't give them her name. "And what makes you think I can help you do that?"

Good question, Haden thought.

"We were told you know the area," Meredith replied. "This man is very wealthy and he's supposed to have a compound here. He does business with people who don't want their faces seen and who can't go to the city."

The elderly woman spoke as if Meredith hadn't

said a word, her attitude changing suddenly. "I don't have too many visitors. It's nice of you to come and see me." She turned her head to one side and called out softly. *"Amata?"*

A young woman appeared at the doorway. She sent a nervous look in Meredith's direction and Haden realized she must have been the woman who had contacted Meredith that morning.

"¿Sí, señora?"

"Tres cafecitos, por favor…"

The old lady faced Meredith again. "Please forgive the darkness. The light hurts my eyes."

"It's fine," Meredith replied. "All we need is information—"

"Are you familiar with this area?" she asked pleasantly. "There is a wonderful history that goes with our town."

"Tell us about it," he said.

"It's a very old place. The original city—on the banks of the lake—was called Tayasal. The Itzá Indians who lived here were very fierce fighters. They came from the Mayans."

"From Mexico?" Haden asked.

"That is correct," she said. "Cortés, the Spaniard, came in 1525 but he didn't try to conquer the island. He knew he couldn't. The people here had never seen horses, though."

Meredith sent Haden a second look of hopeless

impatience, but he shook his head slightly as if to say "let her ramble."

"When Cortés departed, a sick one who could no longer travel was left behind. They began to worship the horse and after it died, they carved a stone statue of it and continued their worship. The missionaries who came in the 1600s made the Indians throw the statue into the lake. They said idolatry was wrong. We have people here all the time looking for the lost horse but no one has found it." She took a raspy breath. "You might have better luck searching for the horse than for the man you seek."

Meredith's face fell but Haden waited for more.

"Tayasal was the last Indian city to be conquered by the Spanish." The woman went on without waiting for comment. "It's important to understand the history of a people."

"You're right," Haden agreed. "If you know where they came from—"

"You will understand how they think." She nodded her head, a small smile of satisfaction crossing her features before it faded. "But things change. By the time I grew up in Flores, it was merely a village, nothing special but there were good people here, hard workers."

As she continued to speak, Haden came to realize the old woman wasn't as infirm or frail as she pretended. In fact, he wasn't sure she was even old.

Between the gloomy weather and dark interior he couldn't be sure but when she'd turned her head to order their coffee, he'd caught a glimpse of someone whose face looked far too unlined.

"My father worked on a coffee plantation when I was a child. Life was hard but we were safe. Then the troubles started. We were visited by the men of *Mano Blanco*. You know them?"

"Yes," Meredith answered soberly. "I know them. My mother was from Buenos Aires. I grew up hearing her stories. I understand."

Haden said nothing but he was familiar with the history they were discussing. In the fifties, the CIA had lent its support to the opposition forces in Guatemala who'd overthrown the president. A series of military dictators had followed. One of the secret paramilitary groups that had formed during that time had been called the "Mano Blanco." They'd cut a wide swath of death and terror through the indigenous communities.

"My father was murdered, my mother raped," the woman said. "By the time they left, *mi familia* was gone."

Meredith murmured something vaguely apologetic then started to speak, but Haden reached over and touched her arm. She fell silent again, her eyes meeting his as he gently shook his head. The conversation seemed bizarre on the surface but he was beginning to feel a purpose to her rambling.

"I raised my brothers and sisters. It wasn't easy," she said in a matter-of-fact voice. "But there was no other option. We had to eat. We had to have a home." She turned her face to the window at her side. Rain poured down the glass, distorting the garden beyond. "We had to have shelter."

The woman lapsed into silence as the door opened and the maid returned, a tray in her hands. She placed the service on a small table between the sofa where they were and the old woman. Handing cups to Meredith and Haden, she gave the last one to the woman in the chair, wrapping her fingers around the cup securely before leaving. The warmth of the coffee felt good to Haden. It seemed as if the house had grown cold.

The woman in the chair sipped quietly from her cup, then she felt for the table on her right and set it down. "The Vegas were good to me," she said abruptly.

Meredith and Haden exchanged startled glances. Neither of them had spoken Vega's name.

"But not Rodrigue." She said his name with a subtle disgust. "His grandfather, Jacobo, that's who I mean." She paused, a slight smile lifting her mouth. "He was a handsome man, too. Strong. *Fuerte, guapo, inteligente…*"

"You were friends," Haden said softly.

She turned her face toward him and he was struck again by a fleeting image of youth, not age. "We were lovers," she said simply. "Then his wife had a son. They named him Salvador. He grew up and he had a son—Rodrigue." She shook her head sadly. "He is a worthless man and he sells misery. He brought *las drogas* to Flores and other things, too. Bad things. I do not like him. I want him out of our town. If you can help do that, I'll gladly tell you where he lives but you cannot reveal where the information came from." Her voice turned to steel. "Is that understood? If you cannot do this, tell me now and we'll stop."

"I understand," Meredith said. "Your help will not be known outside this room."

A small pause built, then the woman looked toward Haden. "What about you?" she asked softly. "Do you make this pledge, too?"

"Of course," he murmured.

Meredith put down her cup and leaned forward. "Where is he?"

"He lives in the home Jacobo built. It's between here and Tikal, in a village called El Remate. The walls are thick and the grounds extensive. His grandfather had enemies, too."

"Can you give us directions?"

"I'll send Amata to you later with a map," she

said. "I know exactly where it is. I went there many, many times." She turned her face back to the rainy window. "I go there still in my dreams."

CHAPTER TEN

THERE WAS A TAXI waiting for them when they left the old woman's house. Someone—most likely the maid, Amata—had called and had the man come. Meredith hadn't wanted to leave without the map but the old woman had been unmovable. She'd probably wanted to call Barrisito and check their story one more time.

Meredith glanced back as they drove off in the pouring rain, her reaction to the meeting a mixture of confusion and surprise. She'd expected someone much younger, of course, and less personally involved, but the woman's motivation didn't matter. As long as she'd given them accurate information, Meredith didn't care why she'd seen fit to reveal it.

At least that's what she told herself. Deep down, the whole episode had left her wondering, the creepy house and even stranger lady leaving her with an uneasy feeling.

"That was interesting," Haden said at her side. "Do you think she was telling the truth?"

"I hope she was," Meredith answered. "But something about it felt...off." She looked out the window and frowned. "Maybe it's just the weather. This storm is getting to me."

The rain pounded the roof of the car so loudly Meredith had to lean closer to hear Haden's answer.

"She told us the truth," he said confidently. "As for the rest, who knows? The Indians around here *are* unnerving. All of Guatemala is like that. It always has been, it always will be. They have their own ways about them."

"You believe what she said?"

"A scorned woman isn't going to lie, at least not about something like that. She wants to help us to get rid of him."

"A scorned woman?"

They were inches apart, the back seat bringing a false sense of intimacy to the situation, the storm outside adding to it. "She was the old man's mistress—he had a child with his wife while he kept her on the side. Would you have liked that if it'd happened to you?"

"She wouldn't care after all this time."

"You didn't answer my question...."

"I don't fool around with married men," Meredith answered sharply. "I wouldn't put myself in that kind of position to begin with."

"We all do strange things when we're in love. You never know."

"I do," she said firmly.

"You're too sure of yourself," he said, his voice quiet and low. "You don't know how you'd react if you had a family to support and no skills to speak of. She did the best that she could."

Meredith looked at him, surprise in her eyes.

"She made me think," he said, answering her unspoken question. "About my own mother. My father went to fill up the car one night and never came back. He left me, my two brothers and my mom to fend for ourselves. That's how we ended up living with my grandparents. My mother was a waitress at Luby's. She used to come home and soak her feet at night but it didn't help."

He stared out the window and spoke to the glass. "It wasn't easy. I'm sure there were plenty of times she must have wished we'd disappear, too, so she wouldn't have to take care of the three of us."

A wash of sympathy came over her and Meredith spoke without thinking. "Oh, Haden, I doubt that—"

He waved off her reassurance. "It doesn't matter now. All I'm saying is that the old lady reminded me of her. You said it best yourself before we even got there. *'You do what you have to…'* My mother *and* that woman did what they had to. You'd do the same thing if you were in her position."

The cab rolled to a stop a few minutes after that. Haden paid the driver then they dashed through the rain to the front door of their temporary home. It was pouring so hard, they were soaked by the time they made it inside.

THEY WENT DIRECTLY to their room once they got inside the bed-and-breakfast. Haden tilted his head toward the bathroom. "Ladies first," he said. "You go ahead and change."

Meredith didn't argue. Heading for the bathroom, she closed the door and twisted the faucets. Haden's reaction to the old woman had surprised her, but it shouldn't have. He'd only proven—once again—what kind of man he really was. Warm. Compassionate. Caring.

She showered, the hot water warming her and calming her as well. When she finished, she grabbed a terry-cloth robe hanging on the back of the door and slipped it on, rolling up the sleeves. It was thick and soft, making her immediately feel better. Drying her wet hair with one of the towels that matched it, she walked into the bedroom.

Haden looked up from the bed where he'd been sitting.

"It's all yours," she said, dropping the towel. "Thanks for letting me go first."

He stood up and walked slowly to where she waited. "You're welcome."

Outside the storm continued, its intensity growing. A streak of lightning severed the sky, illuminating the room momentarily. When it was gone, the shadows felt thicker. Haden lifted his hand and touched Meredith's wet curls.

"I like the way your hair looks," he said. "You're wearing it longer. It's nice."

"It's easier to take care of," she said lamely.

He nodded and a rumble of thunder sounded nearby. Meredith felt the noise echo inside her as Haden's hand slipped around the back of her neck.

"I want to kiss you," he said simply.

"I don't think that's a good idea."

"Call it an experiment," he said. "I've been thinking about it ever since you grabbed me in the prison. Let me get it out of my system and then I'll be able to concentrate better."

"That's not logical."

"Sure it is. If it doesn't turn out as good as my fantasy then I can drop the whole idea."

She knew it was a mistake, but Meredith asked the question anyway. "And what happens if your experiment turns out better than you thought?"

He dipped his head to hers, his breath warm

against her cheek. "Let's cross that bridge when we get there," he suggested.

A second later, his mouth covered hers.

HADEN TUGGED HER closer. She tasted just as sweet as he remembered. Murmuring in the back of his throat, he let the sensations roll over him. The smell of her shampoo, the heat of her body, the taste of her mouth…everything about the moment reminded him of when they'd been together before and none of it was bad.

He brought his hand to her cheek and cupped the line of her jaw, his thumb rubbing over her chin. Her skin felt so soft….

He deepened the kiss and she let him, a groan escaping. Her hands went around his shoulders and she held him tightly.

For what felt like a lifetime but also a second, they kissed. Finally Haden pulled back. If he didn't stop, his "experiment" might go past the point of no return. He looked down at Meredith and spoke, his voice a husky whisper.

"Nothing's changed," he said hoarsely. "You still know how to make me forget the rest of the world exists."

She blinked and started to answer, but before she could speak, someone began to pound at the door.

Jumping back as if she'd touched a hot stove, Meredith turned toward the sound. A second later, she had her knife in her hand and was approaching the threshold, but Haden beat her to it. His fingers reaching for the small of his back, he jerked the door open, Meredith right behind him.

Amata, the old woman's maid, stood in front of them.

Drenched from the rain, she gripped the door frame with both hands and tottered in the hallway, her eyes wide with shock and fear. Just as Haden frowned and started to speak she stumbled into his arms and collapsed.

Staggering backward with the unexpected burden, Haden managed to kick the door shut and Meredith locked it. As she turned to face him, a warm gush flowed over his hands and Meredith's startled eyes told him the rest of the story. Dragging the woman into the room, he looked at her back. She'd been shot. Twice in the back at point-blank range.

Meredith ran into the bathroom, then returned, two white towels in her hands. He laid the woman on the floor and she cried out as Meredith pushed the heavy cotton beneath her. They were quickly soaked.

"Who did this?" he demanded. "Who shot you?"

She moaned but didn't answer.

He looked up at Meredith. "Is there a hospital—"

"No hospital—" Meredith shook her head. "We can't risk it, Haden."

He started to argue but she cut him off.

"I know a doctor," Meredith said. "I'll call him, then we'll leave. He can be here faster than we could get her somewhere anyway."

She ran to the phone and dialed a number, her voice a mutter as Haden turned back to the maid. Her skin was the color of ashes.

She tried to lick her lips and speak, but failed. Her eyes rolled back in their sockets.

"He's on his way." Meredith threw off the robe she'd been wearing and grabbed a pair of jeans. Haden caught a flash of naked, glowing skin, then it was gone. Thrusting her legs into the legs of the pants, she hopped to the bed and pulled a bright blue T-shirt from her bag. Shoes followed. "Get what you can," she said. "We've got to get outta here."

He turned back to the maid, the image of the old lady and little boy coming into his mind. "Is everyone dead?"

Her eyes fluttered open, the effort taking the last of her strength. "No…no one else… They're gone—"

"What do you mean, they're gone?"

"After she talked…to you…she knew they should leave. *Ellos han ido.*" She tried to reach around to the front of her dress but the movement was too much. Her arm fell limply to her side.

Haden reached into the pocket of her white skirt and found a folded piece of paper. "Who did this to you?" he asked again as he pulled out the note. It was the sketch the old lady had promised.

"He was no one," she muttered painfully. "An Indian. Someone he sent. *Él no es importante.*"

Haden crammed the map in his own pocket. "We need to know," he pressed mercilessly. "Try hard—"

Meredith tugged at his shoulder. "Come on," she whispered. "Please, Haden. We have to go. The doctor's car just pulled up. We have to leave before he gets up here...."

The woman's eyes fluttered down but before they closed, she nodded her head in agreement with Meredith. "*Váyase por favor. Ahora!* You go," she repeated. "Go, while you still can..."

Meredith pulled Haden to his feet and thrust his backpack into his arms. He took it because he didn't have a choice and then they were running.

They hit the stairs in the rear as the doctor and Sonia Delgato clattered up the ones in the front.

They stopped two blocks away, ducking into a side street, under the ragged cloth overhang of a bakery. Haden yanked off his blood-soaked T-shirt and grabbed something clean from his backpack. The rain continued around them.

"We have to go to the old lady's house," he said, pulling the shirt over his head. "We have to make sure she's really gone."

"I agree," Meredith said. "But not together. You find us a car while I check out the story. We can accomplish more that way." She looked around the corner of the building as she spoke, her anxiety growing the longer they stood still. "I'll meet you right here in an hour. You stay in the car. I'll find you."

"I don't like it—"

"It's the only way," Meredith insisted. "We've got to get out of here fast and we can't waste any more time."

"But it could be a trap. The only lady could have set us up—"

"If it is, then I'll deal with it."

They stared at each other, the raindrops bouncing off the fabric tarp over their heads, another clap of thunder splitting the air around them. When Meredith had told Haden yesterday that the situation was getting complicated she'd been referring to Prescott's fingerprints, but the description now took on a deeper meaning for him.

He didn't want Meredith putting herself in that kind of danger.

"I understand what you're saying, okay? But we don't have a choice." Surprising him, she brushed her lips over his. "Be careful," she whispered. "I'll see you in an hour."

She vanished into the downpour. Haden wanted to chase her down and stop her, but he knew she was right. They had to get out of town as quickly as possible and splitting up was the most effective way to do that. If she'd been anyone else—any other agent—he wouldn't have given the idea a second thought.

He crammed his hat on his head, slung his backpack over his shoulder and flagged down the nearest taxi. He had the man drive him around for ten minutes, then told him to stop in front of a small *tienda*. He waited five minutes then stepped back into the rain and grabbed another cab.

The second driver was younger and hungrier. His black eyes darted from his rearview mirror to Haden's face. His English was broken but serviceable. "Where to?"

"Just drive," Haden said. "I'll tell you when to stop." He let the kid take them aimlessly down one street and then another. He might have switched again if he'd had more time, but he'd already wasted fifteen minutes. He took a chance and explained what he wanted.

A few minutes later, they were approaching a street Haden imagined few tourists ever saw. The man pulled the car to a stop and hopped out, opening Haden's door with alarming politeness. Chattering with excitement, the driver led Haden to the door of the house before them.

He introduced Haden to his friend, who turned out to be older and harder-looking than Haden had anticipated. The man's eyes skipped over the bruises and healing cut on Haden's temple as he explained what he was looking for. The three of them returned to the cab, the friend apparently unperturbed by the beat-up gringo who wanted to buy a car right then and there, papers unnecessary. He'd heard stranger requests, his attitude seemed to say. At least this one was legal.

Sort of.

They ended up in an industrial park on the outskirts of Santa Elena. The sounds of a garage came from the metal building they approached, air guns and paint grinders, men cursing and laughing. When they opened the door and stepped inside, everything went quiet.

Haden realized why immediately.

They'd come to a chop shop. A very busy one at that.

There were at least a dozen different vehicles being torn apart, everything from engines to bumpers lying around the garage as if a factory's assembly line had gone haywire and thrown them off the cars. One of the workers called out a greeting, the rest of the mechanics quickly turning back to their tasks. From the deference he garnered and the

speed with which they began to work, Haden realized the cabbie's friend was probably the owner.

He took them through the garage to the back.
Haden expected to go outside, but they merely
entered a second garage. It was smaller than the first
but still filled with workers. Haden's eyes scanned
the open area. To the right, he saw a kid changing
the license plate on a mud-splattered Chevrolet
Blazer. To his left, there was an older Suburban, the
fender bent in, the bumper half off. It'd seen better
days, the tinted windows dark, the paint peeled and
faded. Behind the young mechanic, a half-dozen
cars were being worked on.

The *jefe* tilted his head toward the Blazer and
named a figure. It was twice what the car was worth.
Haden shook his head. "I'll take the Suburban," he
said. "And make sure it's got a full tank."

The owner shrugged. He didn't care, as long as
he got paid.

Haden pulled out his wallet, then stopped. The
man, whose hand had already been extended, looked
up at him, annoyance crossing his face at this delay.
He wasn't concerned about selling the vehicles.
They'd go to someone eventually.

"If the local cops rouse me before I get out of town,
I'm naming names." Haden paused. "*¿Comprendes?*"

"That won't happen." The man smiled coldly. "I am
the police chief of Santa Elena. You won't be stopped."

MEREDITH STOOD on the other side of the street from the house they'd gone to earlier that morning. The drapes had been pulled across the windows and the gate was locked. The place already had an air of abandonment about it, but she wasn't about to take the impression for the truth.

She slipped down the cross street and came to the rear of the home. The villa spanned the block, the thick walls that surrounded its perimeter intact. She gave a quick look in either direction, then took a running leap using a neighbor's trash can as a stepping stone. She was over the wall quickly, her landing on the other side cushioned by a thick hedge of yucca. The spiky leaves stabbed her uncomfortably, but she was up and going before the pain could register.

Keeping to the edge of the garden, she made it to the rear of the house, the shuttered windows across the veranda more testimony to the emptiness inside. By the time she reached the nearest door, she was pretty sure the house was vacant, but she had to be certain.

The door opened after a moment's work with the edge of her knife, and she slipped inside what turned out to be the villa's kitchen. The appliances were of the same vintage as the home but they gleamed in the dark, their shiny surfaces as clean and polished as the day they'd been installed. White marble covered the countertops. The refrigerator had been unplugged, she realized; the omnipresent hum was missing, the house as silent as it was gloomy.

Her knife in hand, she walked quietly toward a set of double swinging doors. Pushing one open, she peeked through. Seeing nothing, she found her way to the living room where she and Haden had sat a few hours before. Everything looked exactly like it had earlier that morning, except for the fact that their coffee cups had been removed.

Wasting no more time, she searched the rest of the house as fast as she could, each step making it more and more apparent Amata had been telling the truth. For reasons that remained her own, the old lady had taken the little boy and fled.

The last room Meredith entered was what had been the woman's bedroom. It was large and decorated in ivory, the only room in the house that actually seemed to have some light in it, strangely enough. She looked around then walked toward the bathroom. There were signs of a hasty withdrawal—a drawer half closed, a closet door open, a tiny mountain of spilled powder on the bathroom counter. Meredith stuck her finger in the talc and held it to her nose. The scent of roses drifted toward her.

She dropped her hand to her side and was about

to leave when out of the corner of her eye she caught a movement in the mirror above the sink.

She froze, Haden's words coming back to haunt her.

"This could be a trap...."

Gripping her knife, she turned slowly, every nerve on standby, every muscle prepared.

A figure in black stepped into the doorway. He was tall and strong-looking, the lower part of his face covered with a checkered scarf. She had no idea who he was or what he wanted, but the pistol he held filled in the rest of the blanks. Without a thought, Meredith lifted her arm and the knife flew from her hand.

The man screamed and dropped to his knees, the gun he'd been about to fire dropping uselessly to the floor. Despite the four-inch blade now protruding from his arm, he scrambled to pick up the automatic but Meredith scooped it up and tucked it into her waistband before he could reach it.

She kicked him and he went flat. "Who are you?" she demanded as she yanked off his mask.

He was young and still brave. He didn't answer but she hadn't expected him to.

Grabbing a belt that had been left hanging on the closet door, she tied his hands together, then looped the leather around the leg of a marble-topped table. She did his ankles next. He wouldn't be going anywhere soon.

"Are you alone?" she asked.

He didn't answer this, either, and she kicked him again. "I asked you a question. Don't make me ask it a third time."

"*Sí... Sí...*" he managed to say. "*Estoy solo.*"

"Who sent you?"

He didn't hear her or if he did, he was willing to pay the price. Either way, Meredith didn't care. She bent over and he flinched. When she put her hand on the hilt of her knife, he cried out.

"Who sent you?" she said. "You knew I was coming and you waited. Was it the old lady?"

He looked at her with confusion, his gaze round with fear, the smell of terror rising from his skin. She could tell he had no idea who she was talking about.

"I don't want to kill you," she warned. "But I will."

Something in her voice convinced him, just as she'd known it would. He whispered a name.

She wrapped her fingers around the rubber grip. "Say it again," she ordered.

"Vega," he said, his eyes welling. "He told me someone would come. A man or a woman, he didn't know which."

"And what were you supposed to do?"

He began to tremble, shock setting in.

"What were your orders?"

"To kill you," he said, his voice cracking. "And to bring the body to the villa."

"Well, that's not going to happen," she said calmly. "At least not the way you planned."

Their eyes met in the darkness and she yanked the knife from his arm. He gasped, then his eyes rolled back in his head. He was out before she reached the doorway.

CHAPTER ELEVEN

THE RAIN WAS STILL coming down when Haden parked the dirty Suburban across from the bed-and-breakfast and waited for Meredith. The doctor's car was gone. Had he taken the maid to the hospital? Had she died? Obviously someone had seen Haden and Meredith go to the old woman's house and had known what she could tell them. He wondered why they hadn't been stopped at that point, then a possibility came to him. If the grandfather was still alive, Rodrigue couldn't risk harming the old woman directly. The best he could do was try to prevent Amata from bringing them the map.

Or lay a trap for whoever went to the house later.

Haden felt his jaw go tight. He should have told Meredith to find the car but convincing her to do something other than what she wanted was impossible. He'd forgotten how stubborn she could be. He glanced at his watch and decided to give her five more minutes.

She'd surprised him by her reaction to his kiss.

At the very least, he'd expected her to protest, but she'd turned into his embrace almost eagerly. He wondered why—was she setting him up for something? He didn't trust her but he was relentlessly drawn to her. The dilemma left him confused. Was he falling for her again?

His answer came swiftly.

He wasn't falling for her *again*. His feelings for Meredith had never left him. He'd never gotten over her.

Even though she was a hired killer.

The rain drummed the rooftop of the SUV as he remembered the night she'd told him she was leaving the Agency.

They'd been in bed, the sheets tangled around them, Haden trying to catch his breath, Meredith vibrating with a barely restrained eagerness. He'd been stupid enough to think it was due to them.

"I have something to tell you," she'd said. Sitting up and pulling the sheet around her, she'd looked at him expectantly, her dark hair tumbling around her face, her brown eyes lit up.

"Can't it wait?" he'd groaned, teasing her. "I don't think I can handle any more excitement tonight."

"It can't wait," she'd said. "*I* can't wait."

"All right," he'd answered. "Let me guess, then. You're getting a promotion? You're going to be *my* boss? You're going to be my boss's boss?"

"I'm getting fired."

"Excuse me?"

"I'm getting fired," she'd repeated. "Tomorrow. I can't tell you any more about it but Dean knows—"

Haden didn't want to hear about Reynolds. He'd never trusted the man and by this time, he'd had good reason. The Libyan deal had already gone south and he had begun to suspect why. "You work for me," he'd said slowly, rising from the bed. "You can't be cut without me knowing about it—"

"I'm going out on my own."

"What the hell are you talking about?"

"I can't tell you any more. But it's unbelievable, Haden. I can't say more."

"That's ridiculous," he'd yelled.

A stubborn expression had come over her features. "I can't give you any more details—"

"Can't or won't?"

At that point, she'd crossed her arms and stared at him.

Their words had grown more heated and before he'd known what was happening, Haden had told her to leave. He'd confronted Dean Reynolds the following day, the story not adding up.

"I want the truth," he'd said. "What did you do to Meredith Santera?"

"I didn't do anything to her." Reynolds had finished signing the document he'd been reviewing and looked up at Haden. "She didn't explain any-thing to you?"

Haden had glared at the man behind the desk. "If she had, I wouldn't be here."

"She was fired," he said dismissively. "That's all you need to know."

"On what grounds?"

"Insubordination."

"I don't believe you."

"Check out her employment file. The paper-work's all there. Signed, sealed and delivered." He'd put down his fancy German pen and had folded his hands, his expression smug. "You can no longer use her to make yourself look good. Your star is gone, Agent Haden. Deal with it and move on."

The gray-haired dinosaur had assumed Haden would feel the same way *he* would if something like this had happened. Reynolds saw everything through the filter of how-will-this-affect-me? He'd had no idea.

It'd taken six months for the rumors to reach Haden's level, because he made it a practice to avoid gossip but eventually he'd heard. Then he'd seen Meredith in the airport and she'd told him all he'd needed to know.

She'd become an assassin.

Killing for money, moving from country to country, she hit whoever was targeted for whoever would pay. She had three men who worked with her, Haden had heard, all of them seasoned veterans of one sort of war or another. They called themselves the Operatives.

Remembering his thought at the bus station, Haden reviewed the few facts he had, his questions returning. There was more to the situation than he understood—Meredith had told him so several times—but she didn't trust him enough to tell him the whole truth. The realization stung.

Across the street, a flash of blue blinked through the cascading rain, breaking through his memories. He looked closer and saw that it was Meredith. Flicking the car's lights twice, he started the engine and edged out into the traffic. When he was abreast of her, Meredith jumped inside.

She was soaked, her hair hanging down around her face like smooth black silk, her shirt clinging to her breasts.

"You were right," she said tightly. "A man was waiting for me at the house. Vega knows we're here."

HADEN MANEUVERED the SUV through the narrow streets finding the causeway using navigation skills honed by necessity. Shooting over the bridge, they crossed to the other side and through the town of Santa Elena.

"Tell me more," he demanded.

She grabbed her backpack from the seat behind her and found a dry shirt. Discarding her wet one, she changed quickly, her voice muffled for a second as she yanked one shirt off and pulled the other one on.

"He was waiting for me in the back of the house," she said. "I'd cleared the whole place except for the old woman's suite. Just as I finished that room, he came to the doorway with this in his hand."

She pulled the .38 from the waistband of her jeans and dropped it into the console between them.

"I take it he won't be needing it where he is now?"

Haden's assumption hurt. "I didn't kill him. There was no reason for that." Did he really think she was so heartless? "He won't be using his right arm for a while though. Cuts like that take a while to heal."

"Who was he?"

"I didn't take time for introductions. He told me Vega had sent him and I figured that was all I needed to know. I left him tied up and bleeding."

"Could your man have told Vega—"

"No!" she interrupted. "I've worked with this guy for years. He wouldn't give me away but I don't know about his brother. He bothered me a bit.... There's always Menchez, too," she added. "They obviously know you escaped. Maybe he warned Vega. If he's the one who put you there, Menchez would let him know what happened."

"And Prescott?"

She shrugged. "I have no idea."

He told her about buying the car, the details taking them to the edge of town. Civilization dropped off quickly, the jungle taking over.

She cursed when he got to the part about the police chief. "Do you think he knew who you are?"

"If he did, he didn't care. And it doesn't make any difference now, anyway. Vega knows we're here, so what does it matter?" He looked in the rearview mirror then shook his head. "I want to dump the vehicle as soon as we can, though. There's no sense in advertising our whereabouts."

He had a good point. Reaching for the grip above the door, Meredith held on, the SUV bouncing over a road that had gone from asphalt to dirt. They cleared the rough part, then the pavement smoothed out again, mud flying off their tires in chunks as they hit the blacktop again. On either side of them, the jungle grew close, the greenery breaking for an occasional hut but thick for the main part. As they rounded an unexpected corner, a flock of parrots took flight in the rain. Meredith watched the birds fly off, but she didn't really see them, her mind busy thinking about the possibilities ahead. "Do you have the map?"

Pulling a piece of paper from his shirt pocket, Haden passed it to her. "El Remate is halfway between Tikal and Flores. About twenty miles, I'd say. Vega's going to have guards at some point. We'll have to be careful."

Meredith studied the map. It'd been done with great care, the mileage marked off, the landmarks noted. Vega's home had been placed in the center of the drawing, the village indicated by small homes nearby. A tiny bird was even sketched in near the edge of the paper. If the drawing was accurate then Vega's compound looked to be right in the center of El Remate. Meredith had expected something more isolated. With civilians close, the chances for a serious screw-up tripled. It wasn't going to be an easy stakeout even after they located the place.

"You got any ideas?" She looked up from the map. "I didn't come with the kind of gear this needs."

"There's nothing we can do, but try," he said. "We'll locate the villa, watch it for as long as we can, then go from there. If he's holding Prescott, maybe we'll get lucky and spot him early on. If we don't and it looks like this is gonna drag out, then we'll have to reevaluate."

The road was washed out again and they fell silent after that, all Haden's attention needed as he fought to keep the vehicle from sliding into the jungle. A bus would careen toward them occasionally, but other than that, the highway was fairly empty, the storm working in their favor, at least in that department.

They finally reached the outskirts of the village, the shacks built closer together the farther in they drove. Haden spotted one that had a halfway decent pickup parked in front of it and he slowed to a halt. "I'm going to make a trade," he said. "Stay put till I give you the signal."

It didn't take long. The farmer couldn't believe his luck. Haden threatened him with dire consequences if he didn't park the SUV behind his house for a week and keep his mouth shut and the man seemed to believe him. Shortly after they stopped, they were back on the road in a fifteen-year-old F150 with a shot suspension and bald tires. They both felt better, though.

El Remate came into view a few minutes later. The area was a haven for the backpackers and eco-tourists on their way to the ruins in Tikal but beyond that, the village itself wasn't much. If ruins weren't your thing, there was no reason to be there.

Swinging the vehicle down a side road, Haden parked in front of a makeshift campground, a series of water-logged tents pitched in a grassy area before them. A covered pavilion stood off to one side, a gaggle of teens and twenty-somethings smoking beneath it. Haden cut off the engine and it gurgled to a stop. They waited a bit longer and the downpour finally turned into a drizzle.

They had to find a place to stay before they began

their reconnoitering. They climbed out of the pickup and headed on foot to the center of town, but Meredith drew Haden to a stop before they'd gone half a block.

"Wait a minute. This is dumb." She jerked a thumb over her shoulder. "Look at all those tents back there. Any of those kids would have everything we need. Let's throw some money at them and cut to the chase. If Vega already has someone on the lookout for us, the square would be the first place they'd stake."

"You're right but wouldn't the kids remember us better than shopkeepers?"

"Not with this rain. Plus they're probably stoned out of their heads or getting there. There's nothing else to do around here. They'll all be gone by tomorrow anyway. They don't stay in one place for long. That's not the way they travel."

He looked at her with a curious expression. "Been there, done that?"

"I know how it works," was all she said.

They went back to the campground. The spot where the kids had been was now empty so they picked the tent that seemed to have the least number of patches and called out a hello. The lanky Australian kids that came to the opening weren't as bad as Meredith had described, but they went for the deal faster than the corn farmer had gone for the SUV.

They took the money, no questions asked, then disappeared into the mist. Meredith watched them leave, then went inside the tent and sat down to wait. Haden had gone to find them something to eat.

They'd make their move after nightfall.

"YOU SHOULD TRY to get some sleep." Haden finished the last of the paella he'd picked up for them, then stretched out on one of the bedrolls. It smelled better than he expected. "It's gonna be a long night. Even longer if we do find Prescott."

She faced him in the gloom of the tent, the green canvas throwing an underwater cast on her cheeks. It felt as if they were the last two people on earth, the quiet isolation bringing them closer than ever before.

"What's he going to tell us if we find him?" she asked softly.

"I don't know," Haden said. "All I know is what he's *not* going to convince me of."

"And that is…?"

He opened his eyes. "That he and Dean Reynolds have a perfectly legitimate business deal going and they're just two honest entrepreneurs looking for a good deal. Prescott was there when I was beaten. I want to know why." He told her about remembering two men, not one.

"You think Vega could have been with Prescott?"

"I doubt it. He's not into stuff like that—but he is a crook. And I want to know what they're doing together."

"And your role in this play?"

"I'm in the audience," he insisted once more. "If you want to believe otherwise, you can, but that's the truth."

"And if I find out it isn't?"

"You won't."

His answer shut her up, but it also took away the calm he'd been trying to build. She stretched out in silence on the other bedroll and he turned on his side, propping his head up with his hand to stare at her.

"I heard your father died," he said quietly. "I was sorry to hear that." He'd met Mitchell Santera several times when he and Meredith had been together. The Navy officer had been impressive—and he'd doted on his daughter. "He was a good man."

She took a while to answer and when she did her voice sounded hoarse. "I miss him like you wouldn't believe. I didn't realize how much I depended on him."

"Did he know…what you did?"

She sighed and faced Haden. "My father worked with me, Haden. He was part of the company. A very important part."

Haden's eyes must have revealed his shock because her expression closed immediately. He could almost see the wall that went up around her, brick by brick.

"Don't ask me anything else," she warned. "That's more than I should have said as it is."

He reached across the inches that separated them and touched her face. His touch was soft but his words were harsh and deliberate. "What else could I ask?" he said. "You kill people for a living. That's not a secret between us anymore. I knew the truth a long time ago."

Her jaw twitched.

"I guess I could ask you why," he said conversationally. "Or I could try to find who you've hit, but what difference does it make? The details don't matter, do they? Because you don't trust me enough to tell me the truth."

"You don't understand," she repeated stonily.

"You're right," he said after a minute. "But I probably never will because I don't believe the one with the most money should decide who lives and who dies. That's something for the courts. Or God." He paused. "We're neither."

Her eyes narrowed. "What about snipers?" she asked. "Every branch of the United States military has their fair share of them. SWAT teams have them, too. Is what they do wrong?"

Her question was legitimate and it made him stop and think. Did she see herself in those terms? Why? "That's different," he said slowly. "They're being paid to protect the rest of us. What they do, they do for the greater good."

She clearly wanted to argue, but her expression shifted and she seemed to reconsider. He started to wonder about it; then she pulled him to her and began to kiss him.

SHE'D ONLY MEANT to distract him, but the kiss took on a life of its own and before she knew what was happening, Meredith had lost control, the tension and anxiety of the past few days exploding between the two of them. She moaned into Haden's mouth and let the heat of his body seep into hers.

He slipped his hand under the T-shirt she wore and let his fingers gently trace the edge of her bra before he covered her breast with his palm.

He murmured softly, something she couldn't understand but didn't need to anyway.

She knew she *should* stop them but she also knew the inevitable was taking place. The affair they'd had before had been uncontrollable—it had only been a matter of time before it would return and now that was happening. She *had* to stop them.

But she couldn't. It'd been too long and she wanted him, too, her lies evaporating in the sudden heat that flared between them.

His fingers moved down her belly to the zipper on her jeans. Another flash of lightning streaked across the sky and a second later her pants were off. His clothes were next. Her hands trembled as she tugged his shirt, his bruises and cuts still visible in the dim light. She ran her fingers over a yellowing bruise then found her lips following the same path. Tangling his fingers into her hair, he groaned as her mouth touched his skin. When she reached his belt buckle, he helped her. The rest of their clothing joined the pile.

Haden's voice was husky. "You're as gorgeous as you ever were." His hands followed the curve of her hips, a single finger tracing a line down her thigh. "Why did I let you go?"

She leaned over and kissed him hard on the mouth. "No more talking," she ordered. "No more words. Not now..."

He nodded and the rest passed in a blur. Meredith gave herself over to his hands, his mouth, his caresses. When he paused, she did the same for him, the fire that had been simmering for too long rekindled in an instant. Somewhere in the middle of the moment, she wondered how she'd lived without his touch. She felt like a woman parched, someone who'd lived without water and now she was drenched. His mouth moved over all her secret places and the memory of what he could do to her—of how he could make her feel—came back as he took her to that place time and time again. She cried out his name, the sound of it filling the tent along with the patter of rain.

She pushed him over a second later then straddled

him. It was where she'd been days ago at the prison but was no longer for show. Her hair fell around them as she bent over and kissed him. From somewhere he pulled out a condom, the questions she might have had about its appearance fleeing when he entered her.

The rhythm that grew between them was at once familiar and new, their easy stride building with an urgency. Had it always been this way? Had she always lost her breath? Meredith arched her back and gave herself over to the moment, the feeling an unexpected one, the importance of it hitting her a second later.

She'd missed Haden terribly but she hadn't let herself completely feel how much.

Suddenly she understood exactly what she had lost. And the pain was unbelievable.

MEREDITH CALLED his name a second time, then she collapsed against his chest. Haden could feel her heart beating, his own matching it. Making love with Meredith was what he'd wanted—desperately wanted—but now that it had happened, he realized what a mistake he'd made.

Once wasn't going to be enough.

He'd given in to his desires and nothing would satisfy him again. The need hadn't been quenched—it had been fueled instead and the flames were only going to burn hotter.

He pushed the curtain of her hair aside and stared

down at her. Beads of moisture dotted her upper lip
and he bent to touch his mouth to hers. "Are you all
right?"

Her eyes fluttered open and in their brown depths,
he could see she knew what he was really asking.
*Was this okay? Had they made a terrible mistake?
Could they ignore what had happened and go on?*

"No. I'm not okay," she said. "And neither are
you...."

She wrapped her arms around him and twisted her
fingers in his hair, pulling him to her once more.

Even though he knew better, Haden didn't resist.

CHAPTER TWELVE

MEREDITH STRUGGLED UPWARD from a sleep so deep it felt drug-induced. When her eyes were fully open, she glanced at her watch and was shocked to realize how late it was. She'd slept the whole afternoon. Her gaze went to the other side of the tent but Haden was gone. A rush of alarm overwhelmed her, then she heard his voice and her panic faded. She pushed back the canvas flap and spotted him immediately. He was talking with an earnest-looking younger man, his legs rising like a pair of matched pencils from the sturdy hiking boots he wore.

Snatches of the conversation came to her, the kid's British accent sounding out of place in the middle of the Mayan jungle.

"We did the *Mundo Perdido* pyramid yesterday," he was saying excitedly. "It's really quite something. If you have the time, I'd highly recommend you go there first. It's over a hundred feet in total. After that, I'd suggest the Great Plaza. You can actually see the field from the top of the pyramid and it's terribly exciting—"

He continued to describe the Tikal ruins and Meredith let the canvas fall back. Gathering her clothing, she began to dress, a feeling of urgency coming over her. Buttoning her jeans, she grabbed her boots and slipped them on, her fingers fumbling with the laces. They'd wasted time and let down their guard. What were they doing?

What was *she* doing?

The second question stilled her fingers. Her heart continued its frantic race, though. She felt as if it wanted to escape her chest before it could get trapped again.

But just as she'd told Haden, it was too late for that now. The three of them—him, her *and* her heart—were past that point.

She finished tying her boots, her mind considering the choices ahead of her. There weren't too many of them and boiled down to the essence, only one stood out. She had to ignore what had happened between her and Haden and not let it occur again. How she felt about him didn't matter; her choice had been made when she'd accepted the responsibility of the Operatives. She'd obviously forgotten that—for a few short hours—but reality had returned. She had no room for Haden in her life.

She stuffed the last of her belongings into her backpack then stepped outside the tent.

Haden told the hiker goodbye and came to her side.

"You should have gotten me up," she said. Her thoughts pounded behind her eyes. She couldn't meet his gaze. "We need to get going."

He stared past the barrier she tried to put between them. "That's it?" he asked. "I should have gotten you up? No tender words? No *I love yous*? No *we'll be together forever, amen?*"

She slung the pack over her shoulder. "Are you ready?"

He closed the space between them. "Meredith?"

"This isn't the place," she said tersely. "Or the time. What happened, has happened. Can't we just put it behind us and go on?"

"Is that what you want to do?"

From somewhere behind them came the screech of a howler monkey. The distraction was just what she needed. "What I want isn't important right now. We've got a job to do."

"And we're going to do it."

"Then let's stop talking and get on with it."

When he didn't move, she looked up. His eyes were dark, their sapphire blue now filled with shadows she chose to ignore.

"You're only putting off the inevitable," he said. "Sooner or later—"

"Sooner's here," she interrupted. "And I'm leaving. If you're coming, then you better move quick."

THEY TOOK THE farmer's truck as far as they dared. The unpaved road to Vega's compound was well maintained. Meredith had warned Haden she thought the villa was in the center of town, so he wasn't surprised when they came up on it quickly. Vega had so much land around him, however, the place felt more isolated than it actually was. Haden parked their vehicle in the driveway of an abandoned home, and they went by foot from there, arriving at the perimeter of Vega's land, marked by a heavy barbed-wire fence quickly.

Meredith pulled him to a stop as she surveyed the barrier. "It's not electrified," she said after a moment's study. "But there's going to be more. He wouldn't leave his security to something like that. Especially now that he knows we're on to him."

Haden nodded and they proceeded with caution, Haden holding the spikes back as Meredith crawled through.

Their sharpness reminded him of the conversation he and Meredith had just shared. She'd been determined to keep him at arm's length after their lovemaking and her words and attitude had been just as barbed. He knew exactly why, too. Their lovemaking had affected her just as deeply as it had him and she didn't know what to do with the emotional fire-storm that was taking place inside her as a result of it. He didn't know what to do, either, but unlike Meredith, Haden couldn't pretend that nothing had happened. His feelings were too intense.

He watched her walking ahead of him and recon-sidered everything. There was nothing they could do about what had happened, but later on, they would have to deal with the blowback. Emotional and other-wise.

If there *was* a later, he amended.

They walked for another five minutes, then switched places, the vegetation growing thicker the farther off the road they got. He wasn't sure if he was glad the rain had stopped or not. It made for easier going, but the heat and humidity were deadly. They stopped after a few minutes when Meredith handed him a water bottle.

"We'll have to work fast," she said. "I just hope like hell Prescott's still alive and being held some-where with easy access. If we have to go deep inside, then things start getting tricky."

He drank from the bottle before putting the cap back in place. "If we don't spot him, we need to regroup. We don't want to hang around the com-pound for too long, no matter what."

"You're right. But it probably won't be that simple."

He threw his water bottle into the pack at his feet, then hefted it to his back.

"The only way we'll know is to get there and find out." He held his hand to her and helped her up. A second later they were forging ahead once more. They'd only walked a hundred feet when both of them froze. The sound of voices was coming toward them from the garden ahead.

THEY DROPPED to their knees and slid off the path, the bushes swallowing their presence. Meredith listened closely and tried to make out the words, but whoever they'd heard talking seemed to move on quickly, the voices fading as the sounds of the night took over once more. She glanced at Haden, and he made a walking motion with his fingers. Nodding tightly, she let him go first, then fell in line behind him.

They came to the edge of a clearing two minutes later. Fifteen feet beyond, an electrified fence stood. Beyond it a wide hedge ran parallel to the wire, its leaves so thick it acted as a second wall of defense. A well-worn path had been trampled between the two barriers. The conversation they'd heard had obviously taken place between people walking the route. Rings of orange light spread over the grassy walkway every twenty feet, the tall poles holding them spaced at regular intervals.

Haden pointed upward. At first Meredith thought he was showing her the lights. She nodded impatiently, then looked closer. Small cameras were set on every pole.

They eased away from the fence and hunkered down, their faces inches apart.

"This isn't going to be easy," Haden said.

"Nothing ever is," she answered, "but it's not impossible, either. His setup is similar to one I saw in Santiago a few months ago. Once we figure out the schedule, the rest is simple, unless he's put in some custom features."

"And if that happens?"

She looked at him in the darkness. "Then we're screwed. Nothing's one hundred percent."

He rolled his eyes and started to speak, but she stopped him, explaining the system the best she could.

"So you time the guards?" he asked when she finished. "And the lights and the cameras follow?"

Meredith answered with a nod. "Yes. They work sequentially. When one's passing by, the other goes off. There's no redundancy that way."

"How long's the cycle?"

"It depends on the perimeter," she replied. "The smaller it is, the faster it goes."

"Then all we really have to do is disable one or the other. After that, you use the interval to get over and in."

"It's even better than that," she said. "There's usually a break between the two, depending on how cheap the guy is who installed the system. In Chile, I had just enough time to get over the wall. Here we might be even better off because Vega's compound is so spread out."

"What's the point in having a system if you've got holes in it like that?"

"Would you know there were holes if I hadn't told you?"

"Good point," he conceded.

"That's what they depend on," she said. "Most people don't know. They see the lights, they may see the cameras, they definitely see the guards and then they give up. There is one problem, though...."

"There always is," he sighed. "Let's have it."

"Some systems have motion detectors as a backup. It may not be time for the camera to scan, but if any kind of motion occurs, then it turns itself on. If they're monitored in real time, that can present a difficulty."

"No kidding."

"It's easy to check," she said. "You just throw something over the fence. If everything comes on, you run like hell."

She looked over her shoulder then back at Haden. "It's all dependent on the timing. We have to get that down. Let's wait two cycles, then we'll decide how to handle the rest."

THEY DID as Meredith suggested and in short order, they knew the two guards came at fifteen-minute intervals and the lights quickly followed, the cameras swiveling their heads like tiny birds perched on top. The gap between the two wasn't more than a minute. Haden didn't want to be impressed by her knowledge of the system, but he was all the same.

They went through three cycles just to be sure, then Haden pitched a heavy limb over the fence. They held their breath as it thudded onto the path.

Everything stayed silent and dark.

When the guards came around the third time, they kicked the broken bough aside without a backward look. There were no motion detectors, or if there were, they weren't on.

They waited for the men to pass, then Meredith began to whisper. "I'll go first," she said, "then you come after the next pass—"

"No," he said quickly. "We do it together or we—"

"Then we'll go down together," she said, her voice revealing exasperation. "There could be weight sensors, Haden. Your branch didn't set anything off, but that doesn't mean we're home free."

"Then I go first," he insisted. "If someone gets caught, it needs to be me—"

"No. It *has* to be me," she broke in. "I'm sorry but that's the way this is going to work, Haden."

"That isn't right—"

She put her hand on his arm and stopped him. "I can get out of there if I have to," she said bluntly. "You'd be stuck. I'd just have to come in and get you, and that would only complicate things."

She stood up and shed her backpack, then bent and checked her boot. When she straightened up, her knife was in her hand.

He stared at her and it hit him all over again how much he cared for her. He couldn't bring himself to say "love," not under these circumstances, but the emotion was there, no matter what he labeled it. He put his hand on her arm and their eyes locked in the dark. "Be careful."

She checked the blade, then slipped the knife into the waistband of her jeans. "I will be." She took a step, then stopped. "One last thing…"

He waited.

"If something should happen and we get separated, the best thing to do is to meet back at the tent." She hesitated. "Do you understand what I'm saying?"

"You're telling me I can't go back for you if things turn hairy."

"I wouldn't return for you, Haden. You have to do the same. That's how it is."

"I can't make that promise."

"You have to," she said. "I won't go into this if you don't agree."

"I can't lie like you can," he said. "Take it or leave it."

Their eyes met in the darkness, and he leaned over and kissed her hard. When he pulled back, she touched his cheek, then a second later, she sprinted away.

He told himself she knew what she was doing but he held his breath all the same. A second later she was over the fence. The greenery swallowed her and then it was his turn.

A lifetime seemed to pass in the interval it took for the guards to come back around and the lights to go on and off. The second he could, Haden dashed to the fence, grabbed the wire and boosted himself over. Heavier than Meredith, he felt the barrier sway beneath his weight. He was sure the whole thing was going down, but he managed to scramble over the top and dash across the clearing. The lights flicked on just as he dove into the hedge. Meredith grabbed him and pulled him farther into the bushes, her breath coming out in a grunt. They lay in a heap of tangled arms and legs in the darkness and recouped.

"That was close." Her lips were warm against his ear, her ragged voice revealing her concern.

"Next time, I'll run faster," he joked. "My timing was off...."

They gave themselves a few more seconds to recover, then they proceeded deeper into the grounds. A well-tended yard halted their progress, the grass carefully trimmed, the garden full of hibiscus and birds-of-paradise. In the center sat a two-story hacienda with a red-tile roof and a wide veranda that wrapped around the entire house. The place was clearly old, its stucco walls blending into the setting as if it'd been there forever. If he hadn't seen the satellite dishes on the roof, Haden would have felt they'd stepped back in time about fifty years. A series of bungalows, clearly of newer construction, had been arranged around the larger home. They looked like small guest houses.

Handing Haden a pair of binoculars she'd pulled from her pack, Meredith nudged him and pointed toward one end of the villa. "There," she whispered. "In the dining room."

Haden followed her pointing finger to a series of windows that glowed with light. They were actually French doors, he realized a second later, and they were open, the rise and fall of a conversation in Spanish drifting across the manicured clearing. He could make out a word here and there but nothing more. He lifted the glasses to his eyes but the angle of the walls prevented him from seeing the men's faces. Laughter leaked out the doors into the night.

"They certainly don't sound too concerned. If Vega sent the guy who went after you, he must not know his plan didn't work out."

"The guy's probably still tied up inside the old

lady's house. He wasn't going anywhere anytime soon. But maybe Vega doesn't care." She jutted her chin toward the grounds. "He's pretty secure here. He probably thinks no one would come after him in his own lair."

Haden dropped the glasses and scanned the grounds. "Then is that it? I don't see any other guards," he said. "Or fences…"

"He might have motion detectors and/or weight sensors." She studied the area, then shrugged. "Or maybe he thinks the perimeter setup was all he needed. He could have done that and stopped there. If anyone walks out into the yard we'll know."

"The house has to be wired."

"I'm sure it is," she agreed, "but the system isn't armed if those French doors are open. Besides—" She broke off abruptly. "Look! They're getting up and coming outside."

Haden's gaze shot back to the house as she spoke. Sure enough, the men were walking out to the veranda, brandy snifters in their hands, some holding cigars as well. He narrowed his eyes suddenly and jerked the binoculars back to his eyes.

"Son of a bitch," he breathed. "I don't believe this."

"What?"

He studied the men closer just to make sure, then concentrated on two of them, the third one less familiar.

"Who are they?" she asked.

"The one on the far right is Rodrigue Vega. He's wearing the white shirt and baggy pants."

She took the glasses and stared through them, nodding as he spoke. "What about the guy right beside him? He doesn't look like he's having much fun."

"I can't place him right now," Haden said. "The other guy's the one I'm interested in."

"The one in the golf shirt and shorts? I know this sounds weird but he almost looks familiar."

"He looks familiar because you've seen a photograph of him."

She took the binoculars from her eyes and raised an eyebrow. "Who is he?"

"That's Brad Prescott," Haden said grimly.

THEY WATCHED THE MEN talk and laugh for at least another hour, no one apparently interested in leaving anytime soon. Vega and Prescott had more drinks and their voices rose accordingly. The only thing Meredith learned for sure was that the clearing seemed safe to traverse. A series of help from security guards to maids crossed the space before them. She took a head count, then used the time to study the layout of the house. No one, other than the men and staff, seemed to be present. From their vantage spot, it was easy to label the rooms. Upstairs, she could see beds in almost every window.

Downstairs, in addition to the dining room, there seemed to be a living room and an office, the first filled with generous sofas and armchairs surrounding an enormous fireplace, the second holding a massive desk and wall-to-wall bookcases. The study was washed in blue light from a computer monitor that sat on the desk.

She turned to Haden in the dark. "What do you think is going on?" she asked. "Clearly Prescott wasn't kidnapped."

"They staged it," he said hoarsely.

"Why?"

"To cut out Dean Reynolds," he said. "Prescott told me at the party where we met that Reynolds had way too much money. I didn't understand what he was saying at the time, but he made it pretty clear he was more than willing to take some of it off Reynolds's hands. Plus Desiree told me Vega dissolved his partnerships in 'unusual' ways." Haden's eyes narrowed in the darkness. "I'd guess Vega and Prescott didn't want Reynolds to know until it was too late for him to do anything about it. Making him think Prescott had been kidnapped was the only way. Reynolds obviously didn't know what was going on, but he smelled something bad and knew he had a problem. He had to deal with it."

"But why now? If they've had something profitable going on, why ditch Dean at this point?"

"That's a very good point," Haden replied. "But the answer to a question like that is always the same…money," he said. "A big score is coming up and they've gotten greedy. They want it all for themselves. Reynolds hired you because he thinks like them."

"All that may be true, but I still don't get why he'd order the hit on you."

"I just told you," Haden said. "Dean isn't the man you've always believed him to be, Meredith. He's a criminal, pure and simple. If someone's sticking his nose into a place Reynolds doesn't like, he's going to have them removed. Murder's the easiest way to take care of a problem like that."

"Why use me? Why not just hire a local?"

"He told you why." He waited a beat and the answer came to her.

"He wanted to make sure it got done."

Haden nodded and Meredith returned her gaze to the porch, her heart thumping as she thought about his reply. Looking for distraction, she sent her gaze to the quiet man in the group. He sat somewhat distant from the others, his legs crossed, his face made more narrow by the shadows behind him. He spoke when one of the others addressed him, but he never initiated any conversation on his own. He wasn't drinking or smoking, and something about the way he held himself made Meredith think he found both distasteful. His face tugged at her memory even more powerfully than Brad Prescott's had but she had no idea why.

Shortly after midnight, the unexpected roar of a car broke the nighttime peace. The men stood as a white SUV came into view and pulled under the portico that was attached to the left side of the house. They walked quickly to the vehicle, climbed inside and left.

Meredith didn't lose a second. "C'mon," she said, jumping to her feet. "This could be our only chance to find out the truth. If Prescott's in on this, he's obviously not going to tell us."

Haden started to argue, then he seemed to realize she was right. Getting inside Vega's compound while knowing for sure he wasn't present *was* an opportunity too good to pass up.

They waited for the staff to settle down and ten minutes after the men had left, everyone inside the house had congregated in the kitchen. With the boss gone, they could eat their own dinner. Haden and Meredith let another ten minutes go by, then they approached the open French doors on silent feet. Finding their way to a narrow hall, Meredith motioned Haden to stay close to her.

Their footsteps remained silent as they snuck down the corridor, the odor of cigar smoke still lingering in the corners. After only a couple false turns, they found Vega's study. They eased around the door then locked it behind them, the bolt clicking softly.

Meredith went directly to the windows and unlocked the one nearest the desk. If they had to leave fast she wanted to make the escape easier, but she didn't want to open it now, in case they were monitored. Returning to the desk, she glanced around the room. The walls were covered with photographs of airplanes, the shelves filled with model jets and miniature airliners. She shook her head at the juvenile decor, then joined Haden where he was staring at the computer's screen.

"It's a spreadsheet," he said. "Coded somehow." He pointed to the first column of numbers without touching the screen. "Dates? Names? Pickups?"

Meredith leaned over his shoulder and gazed at the figures. They were a meaningless jumble to her. Haden's fingers began to tap the keyboard as she turned her attention to the rest of the room. A filing cabinet sat in one corner and she immediately went to it.

The labels on the files were all written in Spanish but none of them seemed important. She scanned them quickly, her fingers skimming the labels. Stopping to look at one or two of them, she quickly realized that most of them seemed to have to do with the house itself. There were various bills for the villa and its upkeep, along with the same for two other houses nearby. She briefly wondered about the other homes, then she thumbed through the rest of the folders quickly, noting nothing more. Stepping back to the desk, she saw that Haden had managed to get into Vega's e-mail. She began to search the drawers but stopped after opening the center one, when a file folder caught her eye.

"Haden?" Her mind began to spin as she stared at the cover. "Haden…look at this."

"Give me just a minute—"

"Now!"

He turned at the urgency in her voice then followed her pointing finger. The folder's cover held a photograph of the third man who'd been sitting with Vega and Prescott on the veranda. Staring at the picture, Meredith realized why she hadn't been able to place him.

She'd never seen Abu Zair without his beard and ghutra.

CHAPTER THIRTEEN

THEY WERE STILL STARING at the picture when the sound of footsteps broke the silence.

Meredith dove for the window with Haden right behind her. Just as they hit the veranda, the doorknob to the study began to rattle, then a voice cried out in alarm. Heading back the way they'd come Meredith seemed to disappear before Haden's eyes, the shadows hiding her as she melded into the thick greenery. Haden followed blindly, unsure he was going the same direction but running all the same. He was two steps away from the no-man's land between the fence and the hedge when a hand reached out and snagged him, Meredith pulling him back at the very last second.

Her voice was hoarse in the darkness. "Wait! We have to time it going out just like we did coming in."

"But they know we're here!"

"That's true," she said, "but I don't intend to leave them a snapshot." She tilted her head to one of the cameras. "We have to wait."

Haden cursed and sent his eyes upward. She was right. His gaze swept the area around them searching for an escape route. It went to the tree overhead. The limbs had been trimmed and a ten-foot gap—maybe larger—spanned the distance between the branches and the fence.

Could they jump?

The idea seemed impossible, but it was the only way.

An eruption of barking began behind them, the fearsome sound drowning out the night birds' cries and howler monkeys' screams. There wasn't time to wait.

"Forget your cover," he ordered. "Climb up," he said, making a step out of his hands. "Hurry. We have to jump for it."

She looked at the branches overhead, her eyes rounding. "Are you nuts? We can't make that kind of leap! That's impossible—"

"Do you have a better idea?"

She started to answer, but whatever she'd been about to say went unspoken. They could hear the dogs approaching, their growls growing fiercer as they caught the intruders' scent. In the distance, more howls chimed in, the neighbors' animals growing excited, too.

Meredith stuck her foot in Haden's hand without saying another word. He boosted her up and she caught the closest limb and settled herself before reaching down for him. Grasping her fingers, he pulled himself up just as a black German shepherd reached the bottom of the tree. The dog's jaws clicked audibly as he snapped but missed at Haden's boot. A second later and they would have closed around his ankle instead of air.

A Rottweiler joined the shepherd, along with two pit bulls, their wet growls and desperate snarls the sounds of nightmares. Behind the animals, the noise of men crashing through the undergrowth could be heard, their excited voices a match for the dogs' barking.

Haden found himself holding his breath as Meredith scrambled farther out on the limb. Before he could even process the sight, she launched herself toward the fence. For one long second, she seemed caught in the air, trapped between the branch and the fence, then time sped up and she started to fall.

She caught the wire six feet up, the dogs' hysteria reaching a fever pitch as they threw themselves against the barrier, teeth snapping. Shimmying over the top, she fell to the other side.

"C'mon, c'mon...." Haden wanted her gone before he tried his own jump but instead of running for cover, she grabbed a stick and began to race parallel to the fence, dragging the wood along the wire fence. Haden swore but the dogs took the bait and followed her, the men struggling to keep up.

Haden turned back, determined to get over the fence as fast as he could.

Just as his feet left the branch, he heard the crack, but by then it was too late. The bough that had supported Meredith couldn't handle his weight.

There was nothing he could do…but fall.

GRIPPING HER STICK, Meredith glanced over her shoulder just in time to see Haden crash. Her scream was swallowed by animals' fierce barking, but she realized immediately she had to keep going. If she tried to go back and help him, the dogs and the men would only follow her.

Racing away, she shrieked again, deliberately this time, the dogs going wild, the men right behind them. She thought she heard the crack of a pistol, but she wasn't sure. Dodging the trees, she blessed the fence that she'd cursed a few hours before. There didn't appear to be any gates. If she could give Haden a few more minutes, he might make it over.

If he wasn't hurt too badly.

She propelled herself down the line another fifty feet, then she spotted a break in the bushes. The opening lay just beyond the puddles of light thrown out by the security lights and was almost invisible. The dogs would realize she was gone, but the men might not be able to spot the hole immediately. She threw on an extra measure of speed, then dove into the greenery and rolled. On her feet before she'd even stopped, she raced back the way she'd come. She made no effort to stay quiet—speed was more important. As she ran, the possibilities tumbled inside her mind, making as much racket as the stick she'd run against the fence.

Had Haden been hurt? Had he made it over the fence? How could she get him back if he'd injured himself in the fall?

She was halfway back when a movement to her right froze her in place. She grabbed her blade and gasped for air.

Haden stepped out of the bushes a moment later.

Relief washed over her, and she reached for him, her heart thumping inside her chest. He pulled her into his arms and they held on to each other tightly. Only a second passed before he leaned back, his voice urgent. "We've got to run."

"And we have to do it separately," she insisted. "Splitting our scent will confuse the dogs."

"You take the path we made coming in," he said. "I'll go through the neighbors' yards."

For once, she didn't argue. "I'll see you at the truck." She leaned up and kissed him hard. "Be careful."

"You, too."

Meredith went one way and Haden another. Five

minutes later, she spotted the road. She oriented herself, then headed for the vehicle.

She barely had time to catch her breath before Haden emerged from the yard to her left. He glanced in both directions, then jogged toward the Ford, one arm tucked protectively around his waist. She had the engine running the minute his door was closed and they took off, hurtling down the rutted road in the darkness. She gripped the steering wheel with both hands and glanced toward him. He seemed to be holding his breath.

"Are you okay?" she asked. "When I saw you fall…"

In the glow of the dashboard lights, his face was stony. "I'm fine," he said staunchly. "Nothing's broken. As far as I can tell."

"You need to lose a few pounds before we try that trick again," she joked.

"I don't intend on doing it again."

She didn't turn on the lights until they reached the center of town. Five minutes later they pulled up to the campground. Meredith parked, then jumped from the truck. Opening his door, Haden moved awkwardly, a groan escaping as he slid from the seat.

"We need to get you to the showers," she said. "You can clean up then I'll tape you."

"We don't have the time—"

"They had no idea where we're staying or they

would have already grabbed us. You probably cracked a rib when you fell. We've got to take care of it before we do anything else."

He didn't want to give in, but he had no choice. Moving through the darkness, Haden at her side, Meredith glanced down at her watch. It was just past 2:00 a.m. They'd only been gone a few hours but it felt like a lifetime had passed. She issued a quiet thanks that no one in the campground was still awake. Both of them looked, well, as if they'd been running for their lives, chased by a pack of wild dogs. They stopped at the tent and grabbed what they needed, then headed for the cinder block building that held the showers.

They slipped inside and Haden locked the door behind them.

"Get under the water," she instructed. "I'll get out the supplies."

He did as she suggested. When she came back with the tape and the bandages, he stared at her through the stream of hot water. He'd removed his shirt but he still wore his pants. They clung wetly to his narrow hips.

"What's wrong?"

"That was too close, Meredith. Too damn close."

She crossed the tile to stand beside him, the water streaming over her. "We didn't have a choice, Haden. I couldn't walk away from there and not find out more." Lifting her hands, she put them on his chest. His skin was warm and slick and his eyes darkened as her touch registered. "You wouldn't have left if it'd been up to you."

He didn't answer her. Instead he put his hands on her hips and drew her to him.

"You weren't supposed to come back for me, either," he said, his voice rough. "But you did, didn't you?"

She started to give him an excuse but he didn't let her, his lips wet and insistent as they captured hers. A rush of desire swept over her and Meredith found herself clinging to him, her arms going around his neck, a powerful surge of relief that they'd both survived accompanying her need. The two emotions mixed together inside her, and the only thing she could think about was making love with Haden.

She wasn't sure she could have continued to stand without hanging on to him, but it didn't seem to matter.

He peeled off her wet clothes and then his own before dropping to his knees. She couldn't do anything about that, either, so she gave in and let him take her, his mouth and tongue sending her back to the time they'd shared a lifetime ago. When they'd made love in the tent earlier that evening, they'd broken the tension that had been building between them, but this time was different. This time, he was making love to her. And she was letting him.

She put her hands against the shower wall and leaned into him. Moaning with desire, she felt his fingers slide up her legs to clutch at her buttocks, the water pounding on her back. He groaned, too, and the deep guttural sound echoed off the hard, smooth tiles. Her knees buckled and she slipped down to the floor to where he now sat. Taking him into her mouth, Meredith put everything away from her mind except the moment they were sharing. Nothing else mattered, but this. Nothing else meant anything, but this.

Nothing else counted, but them.

He tangled his fingers in her hair and pulled her head up. "Enough," he said hoarsely. "I can't take any more…." A moment later, he had her on her feet then he was lifting her to him. She wrapped her legs around his waist. Supporting her weight, he entered her, his back against the shower wall, the water cascading around them both.

THEY ENDED UP on the floor, Haden's arms around Meredith, her face buried in the crook of his neck. "What are we doing?" she murmured, her lips moving against his wet skin. "What in the hell are we doing?"

Haden's head rested against the wall. He opened his eyes and stared down at her, his eyelashes spiked and wet. "Blowing off steam?" he suggested. "Relieving our tension? Forgetting our problems?"

Meredith hesitated. She wasn't sure she liked his answer, but she couldn't expect him to really care, could she? Wasn't that asking a little too much, especially considering how she'd pushed him away earlier? "Is that what this was to you?"

His gaze didn't waver. "No. It's not what it means to me but if I tell you the truth, you'll run and hide. That's what you did before and I don't want to go through that again."

"That's not why we broke up before—"

He kissed her into silence. "Let's not rewrite history, Meredith. We don't have the time and I don't have the patience. I only deal with the truth these days. I'm getting too damn old for those kinds of games."

"I'm not playing games—"

"Yes, you are," he interrupted. "We went our separate ways because you went to the other side. You knew I wouldn't put up with that, but you did it anyway. Don't tell me you thought we'd stay together once I knew you were out there killing people for money."

"I can't talk about this now!" Her hands tightened on his shoulders. "You don't understand—"

"You said that before. I didn't buy it then and I'm not buying it now. I know there's more to this than you're telling me so what is it? What's not to understand? If there's something going on, then tell me, dammit!"

"I can't!" she cried.

"Why not?"

"I can't tell you," she said quietly. "Because if I did, I'd be jeopardizing my life and the lives of some very brave men and women. That's all that I can say."

He narrowed his eyes, his words shocking her. "Is Dean behind this, Meredith? Is he running the Ops? Is he running *you?*"

"I'm not answering that, Haden. If you don't trust me, then you don't trust me."

He took her hands off his shoulders and stared at her. "Trust is a road that runs both ways."

All she could do was get away. She grabbed a towel and wrapped it around her, then a minute later, she heard Haden get up. He came to where she stood and put his hands on her arms, holding her still.

She put her hand over his fingers and cut off the words he'd been about to speak. "Please don't ask me anything else," she whispered. "I can't tell you more."

"All right," he said slowly. "I won't ask you again. But sooner or later, you're going to have to tell me the truth. You don't have a choice. I have to know."

They turned away from one another and got dressed, the intimacy they'd just shared lingering in the air between them, despite their argument. Meredith wanted to ignore her turmoil but her feelings couldn't be dismissed easily, no matter how hard she tried. Haden seemed to know that, too, and his understanding of the situation made it even more difficult. What in the hell was she going to do?

She combed her hair with her fingers as her eyes went to Haden's face. "What do you think Zair is doing with Vega and Prescott?"

"I don't have to wonder about what they're doing. I know exactly what's going on."

She dropped her hands to her side. "How is that?"

"Vega's e-mails were full of it. He and Prescott are in the process of smuggling Zair into the States."

"*What?*"

Haden nodded grimly. "They've got everything in place. They're doing *exactly* what Dean told you I was doing."

"Zair's been trying to enter the country for years. There's no telling what he has in mind." She felt a tightness enter her chest at the enormity of the situation. "How are they going to do it?"

"I don't have the slightest idea. But if we don't catch them in time, Zair will be over the border and we won't be able to do one damn thing about it."

CHAPTER FOURTEEN

BY THE TIME Meredith finished taping Haden's ribs and they made it back to the tent only a few hours of darkness were left.

She began to stow the medical supplies into her pack, speaking all the while. "We need to call D.C. This is getting bigger than we can handle—"

"And who do you talk to?" Haden asked wearily. "We can't trust anyone at the Agency. The FBI can't do shit down here. The Guatemalans couldn't care less—"

"Well, we don't have the resources to cover this the way it needs to be. All we've got are the two of us."

"That's going to have to be enough for now," Haden answered, his mouth a strong line of determination. "Until I can think of something else, it'll have to do." He took a breath then winced in pain but the expression came and went so fast she almost missed it.

"We'll be safe here," he said between gritted teeth. "At least for a while. Vega has to know who we are and where we're hiding, but he's not stupid. Until he finds out what we want, he's not going to do anything else."

Meredith watched him try to cover up his pain, and the decision she'd been pondering for hours was made without further thought. He was correct; they *were* on their own and if something happened to them, no one but Meredith was responsible.

The idea of losing Haden again should they get caught was one she couldn't handle.

"You're right," she spoke quickly, hoping she did nothing to reveal her conclusion. "But in the meantime," she dug a plastic bottle from the bottom of her backpack and shook out a small white pill and handed it to him, "you need to take one of these."

"What is it?"

"An antibiotic," she lied. "You scraped your leg when you fell. Normally I'd say ignore it, but your system's already compromised. You need all the help you can get."

He touched the tape she'd wrapped around him. "I'm getting the best there is—you're a damn good doctor," he said with a grin. "Even if you don't have a medical degree."

"I'm glad you're happy with the service." She swallowed at his smile, her chest tight with emotion. "Now take that."

He threw the capsule into his mouth and chased it with the water from the bottle she handed him.

When he finished, he captured her fingers and pulled her to him, their lips meeting in the darkness. A second later, they were both asleep.

Or so he thought.

MEREDITH TRIED TO RELAX but even that seemed impossible. When Haden's breathing turned steady and deep, she opened her eyes. Haden was past the point of exhaustion and as she watched, he moved his hand to his rib cage and groaned. The pill she'd given him wasn't an antibiotic. It was for pain and it would knock him out for a good four hours.

It'd been the only way. He was impossibly strong and single-minded. He always had been, but the fortitude she'd seen him exhibit in the past few days had astonished her. She didn't know too many men who could have handled what he'd gone through and survive, much less thrive. She wondered if that strength had developed because of his childhood, then she decided the origin didn't matter. He had an innate kind of fierceness and loyalty that would be intact until the day he died.

The reality of that situation had hit her hard, but once she'd realized the truth, she'd known there was only one way to resolve it.

Things were too far gone. Zair had to be stopped and Reynolds destroyed.

Meredith was the only one who could do both.

But unless she stopped him, Haden would be by her side while she did it. He'd die before he let her handle this on her own.

Stiff muscles had her bitching to herself, but she concentrated on working out the details, the shadows outside the tent growing lighter bit by bit, the pressure on her deepening.

Finally she inched away. Haden didn't move as she acknowledged the truth. Dean Reynolds had called her because he thought he owned her and in a way, he did. He'd given her the career she had and even though she'd worked hard for it, without his help, things would have been a lot different for her. Her dad had warned her about it once.

"Accepting someone's assistance gives them something on you, Meredith. Don't ever think that it doesn't. They may say you don't owe them, but in the end, payback's what it's all about."

She knew what he was talking about now. She'd taken Dean Reynolds's help and it was time to pay the piper.

Leaning over, she kissed Haden on the cheek, his beard rasping at her lips.

"I love you, Haden." It was safe—she could tell him the truth because he couldn't hear it. "And I always have. You may not ever know that, but it's always been the case."

She stared at him another moment and then left.

HE WOKE UP SLOWLY, his brain thick, his eyes confused. For a moment, he wasn't even sure where he was, then Haden focused on the ceiling of the tent and everything came back. Outside the sun was shining brightly, but the rumble of thunder was already echoing off the surrounding mountains, the building humidity trapped inside the canvas heavy and hot. He looked to his right. Meredith's side of the tent was empty.

He fought to stay awake but his eyes closed again without his permission, a fog as dense as the air settling inside his mind. His last thought was about the pill Meredith had given him. A vague realization pulled at him, but the idea vanished before he could grab it.

He closed his eyes and went back to sleep.

MEREDITH WAS HALFWAY down the road that led to Vega's home when a warning bell went off inside her mind. The trigger could have been the small cloud of dust that hovered on the horizon ahead of her but she didn't stop to wonder about it. Seeing an unpaved opening ahead, she yanked the truck off the road and drove directly into the gap, the tires bouncing over the jutting roots of the trees that towered overhead, the branches scraping along the vehicle's doors. Parking quickly, she ran back and rearranged the vines to cover her tracks, then she scurried deeper into the bushes. From a vantage point behind a huge jacaranda, she could still see the road. She burrowed into the tall grass and waited.

A few minutes later, two SUVs cruised by. They were driving so slowly, Meredith had time to study the men's faces as they passed. They searched the area ahead of them, their broad expressions flat and empty. The men riding in the passenger seats rested automatic weapons against their open windows.

They were hunting.

Meredith took a deep breath and sat up, leaning against the trunk of the tree as she tried to decide what to do next. They'd missed her makeshift hiding spot this time, but on their next pass, she might not be as lucky. She had to move, but where? Vega knew they were looking for him so the villa would be more heavily guarded. He wasn't there anyway. Not by now. Knowing what he did, he'd probably revised his time-table. That's what she would have done in his position.

He had to get Zair across the border *now.*

Forcing herself to concentrate, she thought back to the files she'd seen in his study. Vega had been paying bills for two other homes. Was it possible they could have holed up in either of them?

She had to make her move quickly and there was no room for mistakes. Closing her eyes, she tried to remember the sketch they'd gotten from the older woman's maid. There had been something on it, she remembered now, that had seemed out of place at the time. Something she'd filed away to think about later.

What was it?

Wrapped up in her thoughts, Meredith didn't see the men until it was too late.

One grabbed her arms, one went for her legs, the third one held the gun. She fought them, kicking and screaming but her actions were pointless. Her world went dark, the black hood they put over her head too heavy to see through. It held the scent of cigar smoke.

HADEN STUMBLED to the tent's opening, his mind fuzzy, his vision blurred. Reaching for the flap, he missed the tag that served as a handle and went down on one knee. He landed hard and an agonizing stab ripped through his rib cage. Gasping loudly, he blinked, his confusion dissolving in the pain that followed. He remembered his last thought before passing out again.

Meredith had drugged him.

And now she was gone.

Cursing violently, he made it out of the tent and stood on shaky legs. She was nowhere to be seen and neither was the F150. The possibilities of what might have happened rampaged through his mind, but deep down, he knew the truth before it'd even come to him. She'd gone to take care of things on her own.

Haden pivoted and reentered the tent. Scrounging in the supplies left behind by the hikers, he came up with a jar of instant coffee. Dumping some of the crystals into a bottle of water, he shook it to dissolve them, then drank what he could, the caffeine his main interest. He had no idea if it would help or not but he had to do something to fight the sleep that threatened to overtake him. A jumble of images flashed past his closed eyes with the speed of sound. He drank twice more and a semblance of order began to emerge from the chaos.

He wanted information first. After he had that, he would get transportation.

He found his cell phone in his pack and punched in Desiree's number. Cradling it between his ear and shoulder he continued to dig through his kit. His fingers closed around the pistol she'd given him and he pulled it out.

"I need some help," he said when she answered. "And I need it fast."

"¿Bueno?" she said.

"I'm in El Remate visiting a friend. The one you and I discussed?"

"I've heard he's about to take a trip. You may miss him. I wouldn't bother if I were you."

"That's what I wanted to know," Haden said. "Is your information reliable?"

"As much as any, I suppose." She seemed to

hesitate. "You shouldn't be there. Things could get bad."

"It's too late for that," he replied. "I'm already here and things are already bad. If there's anything else you can tell me about what's going on, you need to do it right now."

"What do you mean?"

"Don't dick with me, Desiree. You know exactly what I mean." He had to push. He had no other choice. "What have you heard? No holding back."

She didn't answer at all this time.

"He's smuggling terrorists, isn't he? From Guatemala into Mexico? From there, it's a short hop over the border to the States, right?"

Silence continued over the line.

"I'll take that as a 'yes,'" Haden said. "Because that's what I think, too. I got a little too close to the operation and that's when I got my tourist pass into the inside of Menchez's prison."

"Your friend's business interests are varied," she replied finally. "Import and export would not be beyond the scope of them."

"Where do his shipments originate? Is he involved or do others handle it?"

All he got silence again and suddenly the game lost its appeal. If she wasn't going to tell him anything more, then he had to make it clear how serious he was.

"You better start talking to me, Desiree. All I have to do is mention your name and you'll end up exactly where I was. And something tells me it might go worse for you in that jail cell than it did for me." He let the quiet build. "Do you understand what I'm saying?"

"He has an airplane," she said after a heartbeat. "He keeps it at a private field near Tikal."

"What else?" Haden asked harshly.

"He always flies at night. If you go while it's still light, you'll be wasting your time. Wait until it's dark and then look for him. He's like *los vampiros*— he only operates at night." She fell silent as if realizing she'd said too much.

"I understand." Haden started to hang up, but her voice drew him back once again. It had changed.

"Listen to me, please, Hade—" She broke off abruptly again, his name slipping out before she could stop it. She started again. "What you're thinking about doing... This is not a wise thing, *mi amigo*. You should forget it if you value your life. Come home while you still can. You were an inconvenience to him before this but now he is very unhappy. If you attempt to stop him, it won't end well for you. I've heard many *rumores*...they aren't good. He doesn't handle disappointment well and he has powerful friends."

"I appreciate the warning. But I don't really give a damn," Haden answered. "And by the time I finish with him, Vega won't either."

CHAPTER FIFTEEN

THE MEN HAD PARKED down the road and doubled back. She'd never suspected a thing. Now they carried her through the brush like captured prey, her arms and legs bound. Meredith cursed herself the entire time. She should have heard them coming. She should have been prepared. She should have known they'd seen her.

None of those things had happened, however, and now she had a problem.

She heard one of them say they were nearly there and a moment later, she was dropped, the jolt making her head swim, the fecund smell of earth and plants reaching her through the hood. She arched her back and reached for her feet but there was no way she could get to the knife in her boots. They'd tied her too tightly. She pulled at the grass beneath her hands with pointless anger.

A car door creaked open and she heard the thump of a latch being released. A pair of hands grabbed her shoulders and a second later she was yanked to her feet. Pushed forward, she stumbled blindly into a fender. The fingers seized her again and jerked her sideways, guiding her roughly. Her hips hit a ledge, then someone took her ankles and shoved her backward. She landed with a painful thud, coarse carpet beneath her fingers, a jutting metal wheel well hard against her spine. She was in the back of one of the SUVs. The hatch banged closed, the vehicle rocking.

The heat began to build immediately but the vehicle's engine remained silent. The men stayed nearby—she could hear them talking—but that was all. Nothing else happened. Time passed and the temperature continued to rise, the air suffocating and wet.

Meredith wondered what they were waiting for, then decided she didn't care. If it got much hotter, it wouldn't matter. She'd be dead.

Another hour went by, maybe even two. She closed her eyes against the buzzing flies and a building thirst to doze fitfully. When a door finally opened and the SUV's engine started, her eyes flew open behind the hood. Four doors slammed and the vehicle lurched forward.

They bounced violently for five long minutes. Meredith tried in vain to wedge herself against the seat, but with every pothole they hit, she lost her footing.

By the time the tires hit pavement and the ride

smoothed out she felt as if she'd suffered a beating as painful as Haden's.

Then she wondered if that was coming next.

HADEN THREW HIS THINGS into his knapsack and climbed from the tent, Desiree's pistol tucked into his waistband. He felt more awake, but his dizziness persisted. The campground swam in front of his eyes, the trees and parked cars moving with a sickening motion. He blinked and pushed the sensation away. Heading for the center of town, he made it to the square in record time.

Record time for someone suffering from a recent beating, a bruised rib and the aftereffects of an unknown narcotic.

Stopping at the first café he came to, he ordered as much food as he thought he could handle and more coffee, hot this time. After the waiter disappeared, Haden turned to the real reason he was there. To find transportation.

His eyes scanned the parking spots around the square. As it was all over Guatemala, most of the cars were ten years old or older, their fenders rusted and dented, their paint faded and scratched. There wasn't enough money for food, much less fancy SUVs or trucks. He stared past the grounds in the middle and the requisite fountain in the center of it. Along with the usual stores, street vendors and cathedral, several offices fronted the street. The vehicles parked closest to the businesses were slightly newer but barely.

The waiter brought his food before Haden could give more thought to his decision. He downed the *tortali* and two cups of scalding coffee in less than five minutes. Just as he tilted the mug to get the last drop, a filthy white 4Runner raced into the plaza. The vehicle's speed would have been enough to get it noticed but the blaring stereo that was audible all the way to Haden's spot on the other side of the church helped as well. Through the driver's window, Haden could see a young man, barely more than a boy, as he wheeled the SUV into a side street and parked. Three more teenagers climbed out, their bold but untested machismo as loud and brazen as the car's arrival.

Haden realized the waiter was standing beside his table, staring in the same direction, a scowl on his face.

"*Esos idiotas*," the man muttered under his breath.

"You know them?" Haden asked.

"*Sí...*" the waiter replied. "That is the son of *nuestro alcalde*."

Haden tried to make his voice sound respectful. "The son of the mayor must be a rich man, eh?"

"He's an asshole," the waiter said with disgust. "He should be in jail. He deals drugs and steals everything he can. Everyone hates him."

"That's too bad," Haden said. Making his decision quickly, he gave the waiter a generous tip, then he stood and headed down the street.

THEY TRAVELED for an hour, maybe longer. Meredith's hands and feet, still tied behind her back, were numb by the time the SUV finally stopped. The hatch was opened and Meredith was pulled out, her ankles untied so she could walk. Her knees actually buckled but a pair of rough hands grabbed her at the last minute and kept her from going down. As they dragged her along, leaving the parked SUV to crunch over a graveled area, an unexpected sound broke the silence around them, the unmistakable *thump, thump, thump* of a helicopter's rotors. The noise stopped almost immediately and Meredith felt a chill snake down her back. The memory of the map the old lady had drawn them returned and she understood. The bird she'd seen sketched in one corner hadn't been a bird at all. It'd been an airplane.

And this was Vega's airport, the decor of his office now making sense as well.

They stepped on concrete and a few seconds later, Meredith was yanked to a stop as a door was opened. A frigid blast hit her and she was propelled forward roughly, into an air-conditioned building of some sort, their footsteps echoing hollowly, voices growing as they walked. They had to be in an airplane hangar.

Someone gave the order and she stopped again, her hood ripped off. Blinking against the lamplight, she stared at the men before her. Rodrigue Vega and Brad Prescott.

Vega spoke first, his voice pleasant and cultured. "I am sorry for the rudeness of your transportation, Señorita Santera, but I'm sure you understand the necessity of it." He nodded toward one of the men who still stood behind her. "Get the beautiful señorita a chair."

Someone scurried off then returned to thrust a hard wooden chair behind her knees. She sat abruptly. They untied her hands, then jerked them behind her and retied them to the chair. She tried to look around without giving herself away. Exactly as she'd assumed, they were in one corner of a large metal airplane hangar, the two men before her sitting in a pair of expensive-looking leather chairs with a rug at their feet. Beside them a small table held a laptop computer, two cups of Guatemalan coffee and a plate filled with fruit and *pan dulce*. The smell of it made her mouth water. They could have been in an exclusive club somewhere.

Except for the fact that she was tied up and they were probably going to kill her.

"I know what you're doing," she said. "You won't get away with it. I've called my contacts in the States."

"You haven't called anyone," Vega answered.

"You can't. If you let Sr. Reynolds know what's going on, you would only be defeating your purpose. There's no one you can ask for help."

She didn't miss the casualness with which he used her mentor's name. Her heart sank as her fears were confirmed. In spite of how she felt, she spoke coldly. "That might be what you think. But you're wrong."

Her threat didn't appear to bother him, but Prescott rose and came toward her. She sat without moving and kept her face a mask.

"You're a very smart woman," he said. He wore jeans and a pullover, his accent midwestern, his expression open. He could have been the engineer Dean had said he was. "How did you get hooked up with Dean Reynolds?"

She looked up at him and said nothing. A second later, he hit her, the back of his knuckles connecting solidly with her right cheek. Her head snapped back and she gasped, her eyes filling as the sting registered.

"I asked you a question. How did someone like you get hooked up with Dean Reynolds?" Prescott repeated.

She looked up again and this time she saw what she'd missed before, his eyes gleaming with pleasure. He liked hurting people.

"He bought me," she said flatly. "Just like I imagine he did you."

He surprised her by laughing. "Did you get your money up front?" His amusement was forced, she realized. He was nervous and uncomfortable.

"If you didn't, you're about to get screwed," he bragged, "because we're taking him down as soon as this is finished. Reynolds is a useless old man, and we don't need his connections anymore. We've got the situation under control and we're putting him out to pasture. He was beginning to be a pain anyway."

She looked at him with what she hoped was a calm expression. "Is that supposed to happen before or after you get Zair into the States?"

Prescott had been heading back to his chair but he stopped abruptly and gaped at Vega. The Guatemalan remained unruffled. He continued to tap at the computer keys, answering only after he finished.

"You don't need to worry about our timetable, *señorita*. That's for us to handle. All you need to do is sit there, look pretty and stay out of our way. You and your friend have created enough problems for us already."

"Haden will find me," she said. "And when he does, it won't go well. He didn't appreciate the hospitality he received at the hands of Sr. Menchez. I assume that was your doing?"

Prescott spoke up. "We needed him out of the way but we weren't ready to kill him. I had some local help."

"I bet the beating you gave him really rowed your boat. Did your help hold him down while you hit him? I guess that's the only way you can get it up—"

Prescott started for her, outrage mottling his cheeks.

Vega's voice stopped him. "That's enough."

Prescott's face flushed darker and he pointed to her, his finger shaking. "You're gonna regret that, you little bit—"

Vega rapped the edge of his chair with his knuckles and Prescott heeled. Meredith couldn't help herself. She grinned at him. "Good dog," she whispered just loudly enough for him to hear.

"Your friend has no idea where we are." Vega spoke again, drawing her attention. "No one knows where this airstrip is located and even if they did, he wouldn't be able to get here in time."

In time?

Her amusement fleeing, Meredith held her breath, then let it out slowly. What was he saying?

"That's what you thought about your compound, too." Her only intention was to stall. The longer she could keep them talking, the more chance Haden had of finding her. If he was even awake by now... "But we found it. And he'll find me, as well."

"You had help," Vega said patiently. "I should have killed Tía Chita before now, but she's old, and she has her grandson to care for. I felt a loyalty to her that she obviously didn't share. My grandfather would have been deeply hurt."

"How did you know we went to her?"

"I bought her maid," he said, smiling as he used her term, but his expression changed quickly. "It seems I didn't pay her enough, however. She turned on me and took the map to you. In the end, her love for Tía meant more than my pesos. She's already paid for her actions, though. She's dead."

Meredith felt her jaw go tight, but before she could reply, a man stepped out of the rear of the hangar and came to where they sat, his overalls spotless, his manner deferential.

"The airplane is almost ready, *señor.* I am sorry for the delay but the part has arrived and my men, they are installing it now."

Vega dipped his head in acknowledgment. "*Bueno,* Tito. Let me know as soon as you can."

The mechanic nodded and backed away, Meredith's eyes following his path as she filed away this nugget of information. Wherever the men were going, they must be taking a plane. Which meant an airstrip was involved at the other end. That was good—an airstrip meant people, vehicles, noise. A helicopter could land anywhere and vanish as quickly as it'd come.

"How much is Zair paying you?" She looked at Vega as she spoke. He was clearly the one in charge. "It's going to be blood money, however much it is."

"Our financial arrangements with Mr. Zair are confidential," Vega answered.

"You don't care what he'll do once he's inside the United States?"

"I'm only providing the man transportation. His actions after that are not my responsibility." Vega glanced at the computer, hit a few keys, then took a sip of coffee. Putting the gold-rimmed cup back down, he tapped his mouth with the napkin that had been beside the cup and stood. "Perhaps that is something you can discuss with him yourself, however. He's requested that you come along with us. The two of you can go over his plans while you travel if you like."

HADEN LEFT the café with Desiree's directions to the airfield ringing inside his head. She'd told him Vega would do nothing until after dark and as he walked, he prayed she was right. He might have time enough to do something in the hours that were left, even if he wasn't completely sure what that something would be.

Swinging down one of the narrow streets, he made his way to the other side of the square, avoiding the plaza. He turned left when he thought he'd gone far enough. The white SUV beckoned, its elaborate front grill dull and dirty in the shadows. He ducked down an alley that ran parallel to where the car sat, then emerged a few minutes later. Leaning against a bus stop, he waited a good ten minutes. Wherever the kids had gone, it seemed they were in no hurry to return. Everyone else steered a wide path about the vehicle, he noticed, except a scraggly dog that peed on the left rear tire.

Edging his way toward the 4Runner, Haden kept a sharp eye turned toward the street. When he was right beside the SUV, he acted as if he'd dropped something. Bending over, he gave the vehicle a quick inspection then scanned behind him and in front of him. The sidewalk was empty. There would be no better time. He scuttled to the driver's side, grabbed the door handle and pulled it open. Expecting it to be locked, he almost fell over when it gave way. Climbing inside, he broke open the steering column with the screwdriver he'd sent a shoeshine boy to buy for him at the hardware store.

He located the wires he needed and connected them, the engine coming to life quickly. Popping up from behind the wheel, Haden put the vehicle in gear and took off without looking back.

MEREDITH FELT her stomach drop. "I'm nothing to Zair," she protested. "Why take me?"

"Ask him yourself," Vega said with a nod. "Here he comes."

She twisted as far as she could in her seat. Sure enough, Abu Zair was walking toward them. He'd parted his hair on the other side and changed clothes, his tailored slacks and starched shirt replaced by a pair of khaki work pants and a short-sleeve shirt, a name stitched over the pocket on the left side. He looked remarkably nondescript. He'd even put dirt under his manicured fingernails.

He glanced toward Vega and Prescott, tilting his head minutely. They left the corner and vanished into the shadows of the hangar, their voices growing dimmer as their footsteps faded.

"Good evening." His voice was deeper than she'd expected and quiet.

She stared at him silently.

"We have a friend in common, you and I," he said. "His name is Dean Reynolds. You know him, right?"

"What if I do?"

He smiled faintly. "He is not a man of his word," Zair said. "I think it only fair to warn you of this."

"You're not telling me anything new," Meredith replied, her mind racing ahead of the conversation. Where was he going with it?

Zair paused in front of her, his nearness a threat she tried to ignore. "We have worked together in the past, but the business arrangement wasn't a pleasant one. He makes many demands and thinks of no one but himself."

"The Libyan situation," Meredith said softly. Haden's guess was right on target.

Zair nodded.

Meredith's voice went thin. "What happened? Did he want more money? That's what usually goes wrong, isn't it?"

"The details are not important," Zair responded. "He did us a favor, we did one for him.... At the moment, the scales are tipped toward us but now he won't cooperate."

"So you got Prescott and Vega to cut him out?"

"They decided on their own to take that route. My resolutions for problems such as these are more personal."

"And why do I care?" she asked with a defiant manner.

He stepped to one of the leather chairs and sat down, crossing his legs before he answered. "You are Mr. Reynolds's protégée. I need him to understand the gravity of his situation. I will do that by killing you."

Meredith's guts turned watery. "He doesn't care about me," she said. "He doesn't care about anyone else. You just said that yourself. Surely you don't think you can control him through me? If you do, you're sadly mistaken. My death would mean nothing to him."

"Normally, I would agree with you, but this situation will be different. He *will* care about your death—" Zair smiled again "—because he will be blamed for it."

HADEN DROVE BLINDLY through the growing darkness, the 4Runner bouncing over the rutted road and throwing him from side to side. If he hadn't had the steering wheel to grip, he might have been out the window by this point. As it was, he felt every bone-jarring hole the vehicle managed to find, his ribs screaming with every hit.

His discomfort was the least of his worries, though. The lights of El Remate had faded from his rearview mirror almost forty minutes before and he had yet to see any signs of an airfield. Desiree's directions had been less than complete. He'd pushed her as hard as he could but she hadn't seemed to know more.

He wrenched the steering wheel sharply, a hairpin curve coming up unexpectedly. The rear wheels began to slide, the mud from the previous day's rains making the road more dangerous than usual. By the time he got the vehicle stabilized and back under control, he'd passed what looked like a barely cleared path on the right. Sliding to a stop, he did a four-point turn and headed back. When the drive came into view once again, he extinguished his headlights and plowed into the darkness. A few minutes later, the orange glow of a half-dozen vapor lights lit up the night. Relief washing over him, he cut the SUV's engine and rolled off the road into some undergrowth. Turning off the overhead lamp, he opened the car door and slid outside, his footsteps silent as he zig-zagged closer. The sound of a revving motor grew louder as he neared, and the smell of fuel was sharp in the air. Two SUVs roared down the road a few minutes later, five men in each, heading back the way Haden had come.

Taking cover behind one of two remaining vehicles parked out front, Haden surveyed the airplane hangar that stretched out before him. A Quonset building, it looked large enough to hold several small planes but he saw there were two other hangars as well. Vega had room for a virtual fleet. When Desiree had said airplanes were his thing, she hadn't been lying.

He glanced around the perimeter of the building but saw no sign of security. There were probably people around all the time, he surmised. Maybe Vega thought their presence was enough to deter any would-be thieves. Since he obviously didn't live here, he wouldn't care about his personal security, either.

His gaze returning to the metal building, Haden

gave the area one more sweep. Then he eased to his feet and sprinted for the nearest corner. Slipping into the shadows, he edged along the metal wall until he reached the front. He stopped there, the noise he'd heard earlier much louder than it had been before. As he slowly peeked around the building's corner, he realized why.

A Dessault Falcon 20 was taxiing down the runway fifty yards in front of him. In the growing darkness the small jet's oval windows glowed with light but the shades had all been drawn. The plane had room for eight but Haden couldn't see who, if anyone, was inside.

He swore with frustration but nothing else could be done. Two minutes later, the small, white jet took off, the outline of its wings swallowed by the shadows of the Guatemalan night.

Returning to the front of the hangar, he went to the opposite side, hoping for windows. His wish was answered. A series of smaller openings dotted the building near the corner. He slipped up to the first one and peered inside.

An office sat just behind the windows, a desk pushed up next to the wall, a chair angled haphazardly behind it. The red light of a coffeemaker glowed across the room. There were windows on the other side of the office, too, and they looked out into the center of the hangar.

Three men sat beside the back bay on a trolley, the door apparently pushed open so they could watch the jet that had just departed. They looked relaxed and relieved, a six-pack of Gallos open on the concrete floor, the beer bottles sweating in the evening's heavy humidity.

The boss was obviously gone.

Haden's eyes swept over the group. They didn't seem to be armed and there was no one else present.

Meredith was nowhere to be seen.

CHAPTER SIXTEEN

IT WASN'T Haden's normal technique, but he had little time and less patience. He approached the men directly, his gun in his hand.

"The first one who moves gets shot," he said in Spanish. "The second one gets killed. You don't want to know what happens to Number Three."

They stared at him blankly, then sure enough, the man nearest the door reached for a pistol. Before he could even aim, Haden fired, the man's leg going out from beneath him as he screamed and fell. The other two froze.

"Okay," Haden said pleasantly. "Who wants to be second?"

The two still standing shook their heads, their friend lying at their feet and moaning softly.

Haden nodded and pointed with his gun. "Pick him up. We're going to the office."

They helped the wounded man up, then dragged him to the side of the building, throwing anxious looks over their shoulders at Haden as they walked.

Entering the office a moment later, Haden locked the door behind them, then ripped out the cords going to the phone and fax machine. He made them tie up the wounded man, then he forced one of the two remaining to secure the other. He did the last one himself with his belt, pulling the shades to the office windows when he was done.

He stood in front of them and spoke. "I want information," he said. "What I don't want is bullshit. If you give me what I do want, things will go smoothly. If you give me what I don't want, you'll regret it." He swung the pistol in his hand toward the man he'd already shot. "I obviously keep my word so let's don't waste time. *¿De acuerdo?*"

The men nodded in unison.

Haden's Spanish was rapid as he looked at each man and described Meredith in detail. When he finished, he asked, "Have you seen her?"

All three began to talk at once. He waved off two and pointed to the oldest man. "You," he said. "Where and when?"

"Right here," he said, his voice ragged. "She was here tonight. I swear by the Holy Mother. They brought her into the hangar and then the others took her and left."

"Who brought her and who took her?"

"Some men who work for Sr. Vega, they brought her. Sr. Vega and the others, they take her afterward."

"In the jet?"

The older man nodded quickly.

"Who's with him?"

"Sr. Prescott." Then he stopped abruptly, his mouth almost snapping shut.

"Who else?"

"The *Árabe*," said the man in the middle. "He's with them, too."

Haden felt himself tense. Zair was with them? That wasn't good news. "Where did they go?"

The man shrugged, a helpless look of fear in his brown eyes. "I don't know."

"I do."

Haden turned to the wounded man. He flinched as Haden swung the gun with him. "Tell me."

"I fueled the plane. They have enough to reach Brownsville. In *Tejas*," he added, in case Haden didn't know. Before Haden could question him more, the man swallowed hard and threw the older one an apologetic look. "Two did take the plane," he said, "but the other two took *el helicóptero*."

Haden's jaw went tight. "Who's in what?"

"Sr. Vega *y* Sr. Prescott are in the plane," he said. "The lady and the Arab, they are in the other."

"Where were they headed?"

The bleeding man told him and Haden's heart went still.

260   NOT WITHOUT CAUSE

SHE FOUGHT but the effort was pointless. Sitting inside the helicopter, her mind spinning as fast as the rotors overhead, Meredith realized she hadn't had a chance. The three men had thrown her in the back of the helicopter and five minutes later, they were in the air. Zair was right beside her, but they'd left her feet untied and the possibility of getting to her knife was tantalizing. Her fear was screaming at her, telling her to go for it as soon as she could. Logic won out, though. She had to wait and be patient. The right time would come and when it did, she'd be successful. She'd seen more people killed by impatience than anything else.

Zair seemed to sense her thoughts. "Your trip will not be a long one," he said. "If things go properly."

"They won't," she said. "Whatever it is you're planning, I wouldn't be too sure of myself, if I were you."

"You aren't me," he said mockingly. "So I wouldn't make those judgments, *if I were you.*"

"They'll stop you," she said, ignoring his remarks. "You won't make it into the States."

"Sr. Vega has assured me otherwise."

"Well, he's wrong."

Zair shrugged. "Perhaps but it won't matter by then. I'm depending on your friend, Mr. Reynolds, not Sr. Vega." He glanced down at his watch, then reached into a leather briefcase at his feet. Removing two headsets, he put one on himself, then reached across the space that separated them and placed the other one on Meredith's head. His fingers brushed her cheekbones, their touch icy and impersonal but all the more threatening because of it.

Leaning back in his seat, he thrust his hand into the briefcase once more. This time he pulled out a cell phone and connected it to his headset. Staring at her, he punched in a number and the earphones she wore came to life, the digital tones of the numbers he entered beeping loudly.

He spoke in Arabic then waited silently as a series of clicks and buzzes sounded in Meredith's ears. When the phone was finally answered again, the voice at the other end spoke in English. Meredith froze.

"State Department, Dean Reynolds's office. How may I help you?"

Meredith broke in immediately, her voice desperate. It took a second for her to realize she could hear but not be heard.

"Mr. Reynolds, please," Zair asked politely. "This is Abu Zair calling."

Reynolds answered a second later, his voice as imperative as always. "I don't know who you are, but you better have a damn good reason for using that name."

"I do," Zair said. "It is my own."

"What the—?"

Zair didn't let him finish. "Thank you for accepting my telephone call, Mr. Reynolds. Something told me you might."

"Are you insane?" Reynolds's voice, full of panic, spoke in her ear. "What on earth are you doing calling me here? Don't you know better—"

Meredith closed her eyes but she couldn't shut out the sound of his acknowledgment.

"I have a friend of yours with me," Zair said. He touched a button on the cell phone then nodded in Meredith's direction. "Say something."

"He has me in a helicopter," she said in a rush. "We just took off from Tikal and we headed east—"

His lips tight, Zair punched the button again, cutting off her voice. She could still hear, though. Dean spoke urgently.

"Meredith? My God, how did he get you? What's going on—"

"Save your questions, Mr. Reynolds," Zair interjected. "They are not important, especially if you choose not to follow the orders I am about to give you."

"No one orders me to do anything."

"That will be your choice," Zair answered. "But if you want Miss Santera to live you should listen. If disobeying orders are that important to you and your ego, perhaps I should kill her now and be done with it."

"What in the hell are you talking about?"

Meredith had never heard Reynolds curse.

"You're going to do something for me," Zair said. "If you do not want to do this—or even hear about it—then I shall get rid of Miss Santera shortly. We can land, I can shoot her, and the game will end there." He paused. "It will end for Miss Santera, that is," he amended, "but not for you."

"What do you want?"

"Your help," Zair said bluntly.

"Or?"

"Or she dies and you will be held accountable for her death...*and* for all the others you have ordered. I am fully aware of what you have been doing and I have reporters at Al Jazeera who have been promised a big story."

Meredith gasped quietly. Zair knew about the Operatives. How could that be possible? Her brain processed the information and she realized what kind of power he held.

Killing her would only be the beginning.

HADEN DIDN'T WANT to kill the men but he needed time. Walking behind them, he tapped each one on the head with the butt of Desiree's pistol and knocked them out. They'd wake with headaches but at least they would wake.

Running quietly from the building, he returned to his stolen SUV and pulled out his cell phone. The call would be a long shot, but it was all he had left. He and Winnie Ceaver had been friends for years. She'd started out at the CIA and then had moved to the FAA. He'd heard she'd gone into Homeland Security, and he prayed he'd heard right. Hers was the only name he could think of.

She answered on the first ring, her voice shocked as she recognized Haden's harried greeting.

"What the hell are you doing these days?" she asked with delight. "Still breaking hearts?"

"I'm trying," he said, "but I've got something more important on my mind right now, Winnie. More important as in life and death. And if you can't keep this quiet, then we've got to stop right here."

"What's wrong?" Her attitude changed instantly.

He relayed what the men had told him. "The copter's headed east, toward the Caribbean. The jet's going northwest. They didn't register a flight plan but according to the mechanics here, they're heading for Brownsville. It's a Dessault, a Falcon 20."

"That's a pretty small jet," she said. "They could land almost anywhere."

"I know," he said. "But the chopper's the one I'm worried about right now. Zair and Santera are in it. The mechanics think he was going to take care of her then rendezvous with the jet." He paused, his mouth going dry. "Is there any way you can track them?"

"What are you going to do if I can?" she asked.

"We can't exactly shoot them down in the air space of a foreign country. Talk about your international incident…"

"You just find them for me," he answered, his voice grim. "I'll take care of what happens next."

DEAN REYNOLDS'S VOICE shook when he answered Abu Zair. "No one will believe you."

"Yes, they will," Zair said confidently. "I have proof. I have photographs, I have information. I've been watching Miss Santera and her little group for years. We've tracked them. We know what they've been doing. The assassinations you've sanctioned may not be appreciated by everyone, even if you have been doing the world a favor by eliminating those who should never have existed in the first place."

A moment of silence passed, then Reynolds spoke with chilling precision. "Ms. Santera's 'little group,' as you describe it, is comprised of renegades inside of our government. We've been watching them as well. Their actions have nothing to do with me or my office except for the fact that we've been investigating them and are about to make arrests. They're cold-blooded killers. The United States does not believe in vigilante justice. When we discovered what was going on, we were as appalled by their activities as anyone."

Meredith went cold. She'd known all along Dean

would have to disavow any connection between the Operatives and the government, but hearing him do it so convincingly—and to a man like Abu Zair—made her dizzy. Dean had practiced that little speech and more than once.

"Tell your lies to someone who cares, Mr. Reynolds. Your involvement with the Operatives is a means to an end for me. I believe you would call it 'the icing on the cake.' I'm merely using that information as insurance because I want something from you. Something that only you can give to me."

"I don't know what you're talking about—"

"I have a man waiting outside your home in Washington. You're going to get him into the White House," Zair said bluntly. "Or I kill the woman and expose what you've been doing. You have five minutes to decide. I'll call you back."

He punched a button and disconnected the call. Yanking off Meredith's headset, he sat back and stared at her, his black stare flat.

"He won't help you," she said bluntly.

"Then you'll die."

"So be it." She shrugged. "But Dean's not stupid. By the time you call back, he'll have a plan worked out. He doesn't care what happens to me," she said. "All that matters to Dean is Dean."

"If you die, he'll go down, too."

She shook her head. "There's nothing linking the

two of us. He arranged for that from the very beginning. It's called plausible deniability. Haven't you heard of it?"

"I have proof," Zair said with a confidence that disturbed her. "He and Prescott have been taking my people across the border for months. It's a small leap between smuggling terrorists to assassinating people. No one will believe he's not involved in both."

Meredith stared at him, her hopes dropping as she realized he was right. Zair had no proof linking her and the Operatives to the U.S. government, but he didn't really need it. Dean's greed had opened him to blackmail and this is where they'd ended up.

She and Haden had been pawns in the whole affair. Hell, they'd all been pawns of someone....

Prescott and Vega had staged Prescott's kidnapping so they could cut Dean out. Dean had sent Meredith to find Prescott, not Haden. She and Haden had looked for Prescott and instead they'd found Zair—who'd been using all of them.

The only genuine thing to come out of this had been Meredith's resurrected feelings for Haden.

Everything else had only been a stepping stone to a deeper level of evil.

HADEN WAS ALMOST to Flores when his cell phone rang. He nearly ran off the road trying to reach for it, his thoughts focused on Meredith and what might be happening to her. He didn't want to think about the possibilities but he'd been able to do nothing *but* think about them.

He snatched the phone off the seat and answered. Winnie Ceaver's midwestern drawl sounded in his ear. "I have a lead," she said, "but that's all it is. I can't say for sure. My contact's an air traffic controller in Guatemala City."

"Just tell me what you've got."

"Believe it or not, a Falcon 20 filed a flight plan with Brownsville about two hours ago. His flight time will be approximately five hours, which means he's got three left."

"And the helicopter?"

"That's a little tougher," she said. "But I might have something. It's not good if it's accurate, though."

"What is it?"

"I only have access to the civil and military airports, okay? There may be private ones out there that no one knows about but I checked with Belize City and with San Pedro, the two civil ones."

His impatience got the better of him. "And?"

"And San Pedro's tower has had contact with a Bell LongRanger."

"Why is that bad news?"

"San Pedro is between Ambergris Caye and Caye Caulker. It's on an island, Haden. If they've flown past San Pedro there's nothing but open water ahead.

The Ranger's a six-seater chopper with a maximum speed of 150 mph and a range of almost 400 miles. If they filled up in San Pedro, they could get as far as Cuba if they hold their breath."

"And if they don't?"

"They'll end up in the drink."

He was at the entrance to the airport in Flores by the time they hung up. Winnie was less than enthusiastic about his plan, but she handed him off to her boss and Haden couldn't have asked for more.

"Are you sure about this, Agent Haden?" The man's voice revealed his doubt. "If you're not and I help you out, I don't think I need to explain what will happen to us both."

"I'm more than sure," Haden answered. "Trust me—you handle this right and you'll be running D.C. by the time it's over."

"Is that a promise or a threat?"

"Take it however you like," Haden said. "Just help me out, that's all I ask."

"I'll do my best."

By the time Haden reached the gate Winnie instructed him to find, a chopper of his own was waiting. He ducked beneath the rotors and explained the situation to the military pilot she'd somehow found as well. The pilot nodded, then went through his checklist. When he finished he gave Haden a headset.

Haden slipped the phones over his ears and they

crackled with noise immediately, a heavily accented voice speaking with urgency. It was the air traffic controller, he realized, from the Flores tower giving them clearance for liftoff.

The young man nodded, and they eased into the air. Beneath them the jungle glowed green, the sides of the mountains so close Haden felt he could have reached out and touched the trees.

Haden spoke into the microphone, trying not to sound too anxious. "What are the chances we'll spot them?"

The pilot looked as if he wasn't old enough to shave, much less fly a multimillion-dollar helicopter with such ease. "We'll find 'em," he said with confidence. "San Pedro keeps a pretty close eye on the sky—they get a lot of dopers going in and out and they're surprisingly good." He tapped one of the readouts on the control panel then glanced at Haden. "I'm not too bad in situations like this," he bragged with a grin. "I promise I won't let you down…."

Haden ignored the kid's joke and hoped his confidence was justified. They flew for another ten minutes, then the pilot spoke.

"There it is."

His voice was so low-key Haden didn't understand the importance of what he'd said until he pointed to the empty sky in front of them and repeated himself. A light reached out from the darkness, its pinpoint motion shaky. "That must be your target," he said. "It's exactly where the controller said it would be if it maintained its course and speed...."

Haden's pulse began to pound, the sound so loud it took precedence over the thumping rotors overhead. "Are you sure?"

"Looks like it from here," he answered, "but in another minute, I'll know for sure. Hang tight."

As he gave his warning, he revved the helicopter's engine to its maximum, the pistol-grip controls firmly in hand. At least, that's how Haden interpreted the increase in noise that seemed to consume them with its ferocity. When he felt his body thud against the seat as they shot forward, he knew he'd been right. In a minute or less, the chopper ahead of them took shape, the long, sleek nose gleaming in the strobelike flash of its rotating lights.

MEREDITH LOOKED OUT the chopper's window and felt a ripple of shock. They'd left the island and reached the coastline and she hadn't realized it. The water beneath them gleamed in the dark as the lights of the beach faded. They were barely above the waves. The combination of low altitude and high speed made her dizzy, but when she heard a ringing in her headset, she put her reaction aside. Dean's secretary answered as quickly as she had before.

"Mr. Reynolds, please."

"I'm sorry, he's not in," she said nervously. "Could I, um, take a message?"

Meredith watched Zair's expression go ugly. "What do you mean, he's not in? He knew I was going to call him at this time—"

"He had to step out," she said. "I—I'm sure he'll be right back—"

Zair punched a button on the side of his phone and ripped off his headset. The cabin was too small for him to stand but he tried anyway, his head brushing the ceiling of the chopper, forcing him to hunch. Rage lit his eyes and without any warning at all, he slapped Meredith. Before she could right herself, he hit her again.

"Do you see what a coward your friend is?" His scream rang out above the noise of the engines but even if she'd been unable to hear him, Meredith would have understood. "He can hide but he won't be able to stop me. It will not be easy but I can do what I want without his help."

The chopper took a dip and he grabbed for a strap, catching himself at the last minute. Whirling, he cried out at the pilot. "What are you doing, you idiot? Can't you control this machine? Who taught you to fly?"

The tirade continued, but Meredith didn't bother to listen. Squirming in her seat, she bent over. Before she could grab her knife, Zair turned back. He yelled at her and reached out, but he missed, his fingers brushing her hair just as the helicopter bounced again.

Her father had been a pilot and his voice spoke in Meredith's ear. They were flying too low, the hot currents coming off the warm Caribbean filling their airspace with turbulence. Meredith had a second to wonder why the pilot didn't know that before the chopper dropped with a sickening jolt.

"THAT'S YOUR TARGET," the pilot confirmed. "Long-Ranger Six Five Bravo Papa."

Haden squinted through the darkness at the numbers painted on the chopper just above the door but before he could read them, the helicopter dipped drastically to the right.

"Whoa!" They continued to watch, then the aircraft took another stomach-churning drop before tilting radically in the opposite direction.

Haden winced as he imagined what that must have felt like from the inside of the helicopter. "What the hell's going on?"

"I don't have a clue," the pilot answered. "But I'm glad we're not in there with 'em."

HER ARM SOCKETS SHRIEKED as she stretched out again, but the pain didn't matter when her fingers found her heel. Punching the side of the shoe, Meredith felt the catch give way and a second later her knife was in her hand. She turned it around and hacked blindly at the ties on her wrist. The blade cut without discretion, slicing her skin as well as the ropes, but she barely felt the sting.

Zair's eyes widened when he realized what she was doing. Lurching toward her, he snatched at her arm, his fingernails raking her as the aircraft tilted forty-five degrees. He fell with a crash and bounced against the door of the cabin, screaming as he hit it with a thud.

His fall gave her just enough time. The rope around her wrists fell free, and Meredith wasted no time in jumping on top of him. Their faces were inches apart, Zair's gaze murderous as he went for her hand. She twisted backward and he missed the knife she clutched, but his other hand wrapped itself about her throat with surprising strength.

The confines of the cabin forced a viciousness on them both. He tightened his fingers, but she thrust her knee into his crotch, and his grip loosened momentarily, a stream of invective spewing from his lips. Yanking her arm from his hand, she freed herself and brought the knife down with a slash, stabbing him in the chest, then drawing the blade up before she pulled it out. His eyes went wide and he gasped, but as she leaned over to do it again, he reached for something behind him.

She didn't realize what he'd done until the door of the chopper flew open. She screamed, but the wind sucked the sound from her lungs.

He grabbed her by the collar of her shirt and flipped her into the empty air.

CHAPTER SEVENTEEN

"Oh, shit!" Haden's heart stopped in midbeat. "Do you see her? Where'd she go? He threw her out, for Christ's sake! We've got to find her!"

"Stay loose, man, stay loose!"

"*You* stay loose," Haden screamed. "Get this chopper down there right now or by God, I'll—"

His sentence went unfinished. Gripping the controls, the pilot pitched the helicopter down at an angle Haden wouldn't have thought possible. A second later, they were inches above the water.

And Meredith was nowhere to be seen.

Haden started to open the door beside his seat, but the pilot pulled him back. "Hang on," he cried. "I've got pontoons, man. I can get us there—just give me a second."

The aircraft landed on the water's surface, but Haden didn't wait. He jumped feetfirst and started swimming in an ever-widening circle. He'd made two laps and was on his third when the pilot's voice reached him.

"Go right!" He shone a spotlight ahead of Haden, ten or fifteen yards. "She's at your three o'clock. I can see her!"

Haden changed his direction, his arms pulling at the current, the water cooler than he'd expected. He felt as if he were struggling through a darkness that had no start and no end, a nightmare that stretched forever. His chest began to ache.

"Keep going," the pilot yelled behind him. "You're almost to her!"

Haden pushed harder and finally caught a flash of white. The sight spurred him on to Meredith's side.

Her eyes were closed, her face waxy. He thought the worst, then realized she was still breathing. He hooked his arm around her chest and started swimming.

He made it back to the chopper in record time, the pilot leaning out to help him. The two of them pulled Meredith in together. They stretched her out on the floor of the cabin and she started to cough, a flood of seawater erupting from her. A knot in his throat, Haden wiped Meredith's face as the pilot jumped back in his seat and they took off again.

Meredith moaned and got out a single word. "Zair?"

"Forget him—"

"I…I stabbed him." She winced in pain. "Got to stop Reynolds—"

He put his finger over her lips and tried to stop

her from talking but Meredith persisted. Explaining what Zair wanted Dean Reynolds to do took the last of her energy. Her eyes were shutting even as Haden went for his cell phone.

Winnie Ceaver's boss sounded delighted—and relieved. "I'll take care of Reynolds and the man who's waiting at his house, Agent Haden," he promised. "And when you get back to D.C., let me know. I'll buy you a beer."

Haden ended the call and faced Meredith again. He wasn't sure he'd ever be able to erase the image lodged in his mind of her in a free fall from a hovering helicopter. The pilot had been correct—she hadn't had that far to go—and Haden knew all the statistics—he'd had them drilled into his head during his service but the phrase *terminal velocity* wouldn't leave him regardless. A few more feet of altitude, a different angle, a flat sea instead of waves? Who knew what might have happened... Haden shut down his brain at that point. He couldn't let himself think of the alternatives.

An ambulance was waiting on the tarmac when they landed. They pulled under the porte cochere of the hospital in Belize City ten minutes after that.

WHEN MEREDITH OPENED her eyes, she knew she was in a hospital but she had no memory of getting there. The last thing her brain had recorded was the pleasure on Abu Zair's face as he'd thrown her out the open helicopter door. She shuddered violently and the man standing beside her bed put his hand on her arm. His name tag read Dr. Caesar.

"Easy does it." He spoke in English, his accent colored with a soft Caribbean lilt. "You're safe now."

She looked into his warm brown eyes and hoped that he was right. Her voice sounded rusty when she spoke. "How long…have I been…out?"

He glanced at his watch, then made a note on the chart he held. "Four hours, seventeen minutes."

"Am I…okay?"

"We're waiting on some X-rays but you appear to be fit as a fiddle." He grinned as if he enjoyed using the cliché. Which, he probably did. "Someone in lesser shape might not have survived the fall, but you're a very strong woman and it wasn't a very long distance. Plus you were retrieved very quickly. That definitely helped."

"By…Haden?" she croaked.

"Haden? Might that be the man who's refused to leave no matter how much we've told him to go?" He jerked his thumb behind him. Through an uncovered window she saw a nurse's station and a man dozing in a nearby office chair. "That one?"

She nodded, even though it hurt.

"I'll get him," the white-coated doctor said. "Then perhaps I can reclaim my chair."

She watched through the window as he strode up to Haden and touched him gently on the shoulder. Haden blinked into awareness as the doctor spoke, then leapt from the chair so fast, it spun behind him. A nurse coming around the corner caught it, but neither of them noticed as Haden entered Meredith's room and came directly to her bedside.

Both of them seemed overwhelmed, the reality of what could have been stealing everything, including their voices. They stared at each other in silence, then Meredith finally spoke. "Has Dean been picked up?"

He'd expected something else, she realized a second too late, but Haden answered her and she stopped wondering what he'd wanted to hear.

"I don't know," he said. "I got the info to Homeland Security. It's up to them now."

"What about Zair?"

"No."

"Damn…"

"He fell out right after you did. The pilot was trying to help you—that's why he was jerking the chopper all over hell and back. Turns out he wasn't a fan of Zair's to start with. When he started slapping you around, the pilot got fed up. I didn't see Zair go out, but the guy flying my chopper told me he saw it."

She couldn't help but smile, her father's voice coming into her ear. "I wondered about that sudden turbulence. I'll have to be sure and thank the pilot."

"I already did, believe me."

"What about the plane? Vega and Prescott are in it."

Haden gripped the railing of the bed as he nodded. "Homeland's been advised about them, too, as well as the FAA and the border patrol. They know what they're flying and where they're headed. I had a chat with the mechanics at Vega's hangar. Zair was going to rendezvous with them in Brownsville."

"Zair called Dean while we were in the air. He was definitely involved from the very beginning, Haden. Dean sent me down here to track down Prescott. He ordered the hit on you because he thought you'd lead me to Prescott, that's all. Everything was a coverup. Everyone was lying." The silence built between them again. Meredith broke it this time as well. "It hardly seems fair, does it?"

"What do you mean?"

"I came down here to take your life but you end up saving mine. How ironic is that?"

"It was meant to be."

Her heart tripped. "You think so?"

"There's no other way to explain it," he said. "Unless one of us can admit to the truth."

"And what would that be?"

"That we love each other."

The words were the ones she wanted to hear, but something in his voice was off. Her throat began to close and all she could do was stare at him.

"Is that so awful?" she whispered.

He tortured her. Turning away, he walked to the window that looked out at the nurse's station. Staring out for a moment, he seemed to be making a decision, then he came back to the edge of the bed.

"I'll love you until the day I die." He stopped, took a breath, then spoke again. "But you don't trust me, Meredith. At least not enough to tell me the truth. And that isn't the way things are supposed to happen."

She felt as if she was falling again, her body tumbling through the bottomless black night one more time, no end in sight. She couldn't breathe or speak. She finally managed to regain some control. "You don't know the whole story, Haden."

"I know you kill people and I suspect Dean's behind the Ops. I want to hear the truth from your lips, though, Meredith. I want you to explain it. If you can't, then we don't have what it takes for this relationship to work."

She blinked. She couldn't tell him the truth but if she didn't, she'd lose him again. The first time had been painful enough—she wasn't sure she could survive a second time. "You used to say the needs of the many outweighed the desires of the few." She edged around the issue, her eyes begging him to understand. "Don't you still think that?"

"Whether I do or not, it doesn't matter."

"I took a vow and I have to honor that." She

realized she was gripping his hand. She had no idea how or when she'd reached for it. "No matter how much I love you, I can't change who I am, Haden. What I do—and *why*—I do it are part of that." She raised his fingers to her mouth and pressed her lips against his skin. Inhaling his scent, she tried to save the memory, then released his fingers. Her voice broke when she spoke. "I can't walk away from who I am."

"I know," he said tenderly. "But neither can I. No matter how much I love you."

THEY ARRIVED in Washington two days later, the trip and all that followed a nightmare for Haden. He desperately wanted to take Meredith into his arms and pretend he didn't care, but he just couldn't make himself do it. He loved her—he *knew* he loved her—but deep down he also knew a commitment that was only half shared would never work out.

Their briefings passed in a blur, Haden giving up the details of everything that had happened, Meredith, he assumed, doing the same. By the time it was over, they both ended up with hero labels. He didn't care. All Haden wanted was a shot at Dean Reynolds.

Haden got his wish the day after Meredith went back to Miami. His new best friend in Homeland Security, Winnie's boss, arranged the meeting as a favor. "Hell, I owe you something," he'd replied when Haden had requested the meeting. "I just reeled in a damn big fish, thanks to you giving me the bait."

A bright-eyed younger agent, suited and starched, drove Haden to the prison where Reynolds was being held just over the Maryland border. The day was rainy and dark. He seemed anxious to pick Haden's brain but Haden didn't cooperate. The kid finally got the message and quit trying but they were halfway to Delaware before it soaked in.

They parked and Haden left the car without bothering to look back. He walked directly to the warden's office. The phone calls had already been made and the explanations given. The flinty eyed man behind the wooden desk shook Haden's hand then turned him over to an underling who led him to a private conference room. Haden wondered about the other prisoners, but he didn't bother to ask. He wouldn't have gotten any answers anyway.

Reynolds shuffled in five minutes later, his hands shackled, his expression laced with resentment. Glaring at Haden, he sat down in the chair on the other side of the table. The guard clipped his handcuffs to a ring underneath the metal table, then dipped his head in Haden's direction. "I'll be outside. If you need me, tap the window."

The door closed behind him. Haden met Reynolds's cold eyes and spoke. "How do you like your new home? I hope it's comfortable. You're gonna be here for a while."

"What do you want?"

"The truth," Haden said. "It's a simple request. Think you can handle it?"

"You're the one who can't handle it." The older man's voice was as haughty as ever. "Why should I give it to you, anyway? All you did was screw things up. I was doing my job," he said. "I was protecting the country. You wouldn't understand even if I did explain."

"Save it for the lawyers," Haden said wearily. "I don't want your excuses and I don't give a damn about your defense. They can lock your ass up for the next hundred years for all I care."

"Is that how Meredith feels, too?"

Haden blinked. "What do you care? She nearly died doing your bidding. You ought to hang just for what you put her through."

"She's a good agent," he said, his voice gruff. "She was made for the job I gave her."

"Which job are you talking about, Reynolds?" Haden asked. "The one where she does your dirty work or the one where her hits are sanctioned?"

The old man's shoulders went rigid then his eyes darted past Haden's only to return a second later.

Haden leaned across the table, his gaze never

leaving the former director's. "I know she's a killer," Haden said bluntly. "But does she do it just for you? She wouldn't tell me the truth."

Reynolds licked his lips nervously and Haden leaned even closer. The other man flinched.

"Tell me," Haden demanded, "or your life, as bad as it is, will get a hell of a lot worse."

"Meredith works on direct orders from the president of the United States. She isn't a paid killer. She's still an agent."

Haden stared at Reynolds in shock, her words echoing in his mind. *"You just don't understand."* Meredith had been right. He'd figured out part of it, but obviously not everything. This went up to the President?

"Ever heard of Black Box?" Reynolds's voice brought Haden back. "It's a classification so deep most people don't even know it exists, much less who the players are. She's one of them."

Haden stood, his palms flat against the table that separated them.

"I've run her and her group ever since she got 'fired.' The whole thing was a setup."

"Her hits—"

"—were all sanctioned," Reynolds said. "She's been operating at the pleasure of the United States government and with the consent of every government whose citizens were 'involved.'"

"She wouldn't tell me."

"Of course she wouldn't," Reynolds said simply. "Meredith's a good girl. She plays by the rules. That's why she agreed to go after you. I told her you'd turned and were smuggling terrorists into the country. She never questioned me."

"Even though it cost her."

Reynolds met Haden's gaze. "Even though it cost her."

A heavy silence built between them. Haden broke it. "You knew about us, didn't you?"

Reynolds nodded once.

"Didn't you worry she might have second thoughts about hitting me?"

"It never crossed my mind because I didn't think she'd ever loved you." He paused. "I see now that was my biggest mistake."

SHE'D BEEN BACK in Miami for almost six weeks when the call came.

"My name is Lucy Quinlen. I'm phoning from the White House for Meredith Santera."

Meredith gripped the telephone against her ear. "This is Meredith."

"Hello, Miss Santera. I'm sorry to disturb you. I know you're taking a hiatus, but the president wanted me to see if you might be available for a private lunch with him next Friday. Only the two of you would be present. Are you free?"

Meredith swallowed. "Absolutely. I'd be delighted."

"Good," she said briskly. "We'll see you at noon. Someone will call you on Wednesday with details regarding your transportation and arrival arrangements. Again, this is not a public event."

Meredith put the phone down on the table beside her and shook her head, the woman's message clear. The president wanted to acknowledge Meredith's actions but at the same time keep her cover intact. She should have been amazed—getting a call from the White House wasn't an everyday occurrence for her—but then again, nothing had been normal since she'd returned. Classified debriefings, hidden meetings, secret appointments... That's all she'd done for the past few weeks and they'd merged into a fog of prying questions and buried details. Only one detail remained sharp and she couldn't get it out of her mind.

Haden's face haunted her. Everywhere she went, she thought she saw him. Every time the doorbell rang, she hoped he was standing on the other side. When the phone sounded, her heart would stop.

They'd flown back to the States on a military plane then he'd disappeared after their debriefings in D.C. From the steps of the capital, she'd watched the crowds at the Mall absorb him, then she'd gone the opposite direction, her heart going with him, her body heading the other way.

A week passed before she realized she was in mourning, the emotion wrapping itself around her as deeply as it had when she'd lost her father. She'd had no choice in giving up her dad. Haden could still be hers if she would only tell him the truth.

Even the satisfaction of knowing Prescott and Vega had been picked up in Brownsville didn't help. Zair's body had never been found but Meredith was certain he was dead. She'd mortally wounded him with her knife and she knew that for a fact. She'd had the pleasure of telling Dean Reynolds so when she'd visited him one day. Other than that, their meeting had been strangely empty. The hurt she felt over her mentor's behavior was nothing compared to the pain she felt over losing Haden once more. In the long run, maybe that was a good thing. It had definitely taken her mind away from Reynolds's betrayal.

Going into the kitchen she opened the refrigerator and pulled out a bottle of water. She twisted the cap off and drank but her throat stayed tight.

The loyalty she felt for her country and the sense of duty that was ingrained in her had never been tested as severely as it had been over the past few weeks. At least once a day, she'd found herself picking up the phone to call Haden, but all she had to do was think about Dean Reynolds and she'd put the phone down again.

Service to your country meant just that. Everyone, including yourself, came in a distant second. She'd realized that when she'd started the Operatives. Now her commitment was being tested. She had to stand firm—too many lives depended on it.

Her heart would heal. Eventually.

It had to, right?

HE WAS STANDING in the southeast corner of Lafayette Park when Meredith walked out. She didn't see him, which was exactly what he wanted, and Haden used the time to study her. She'd lost some weight, but she looked incredible, her dark hair framing her face, her white suit trim and fitted. He tensed his shoulders for a second, then he forced himself to relax. If he got uptight now, he'd blow it—just like he had six weeks ago.

She crossed the street and headed for the park, her eyes scanning the ever-present crowd of tourists as if she could feel his stare. Feeling foolish, he ducked behind a tree then continued down the sidewalk until he was behind her.

She walked deeper into the square, her steps slow and easy, her stride unhurried. He knew where she'd been and what she'd been doing, but she didn't look nervous. Watching her stroll so casually, no one would have guessed she'd just come from talking to the president of the United States.

No one would have guessed she was an assassin for her country, either.

No one including Haden.

But now he knew the truth.

He waited until she was close to the other side of the park, then he began to cross the grass. The crowds parted, then came together, but he kept her in sight, the flash of her white suit coming and going. He was almost to the opposite corner when he realized the snowy jacket he'd been following was now on the shoulders of a much older woman. He had already raised his hand to stop her but let his fingers fall to his side when the stranger turned and stared at him, her mouth firmly set in a line of disapproval.

With a muttered curse he went back the way he'd come.

Someone tapped his shoulder a second later. He pivoted, his hand at his waist, then froze. Meredith stood before him.

"Looking for someone?" she asked.

"What the hell are you doing?" He shook his head. "I thought that was you—"

"I know what you thought," she answered. "It cost me a three-hundred dollar jacket to be sure, but I wanted to see if you were actually going to approach me or not. I wasn't certain..." Her sentence drifted off.

"You could have stopped and waited for me."

"You know me." She grinned. "That would have been too easy. I always have to complicate things instead."

"That's the truth."

They stared at each other, the tourists moving around the island they formed.

"Can we sit down?" Haden finally asked. "I'd like to talk to you, if you've got the time."

She hesitated but only for a second. "I'm on vacation," she answered. "Why not?"

They made their way to the nearest park bench and sat, the White House forming a stately backdrop. Haden glanced toward it and realized how appropriate their position was.

He turned back to Meredith and wasted no time. The not-knowing was the worst part. He had to get it over with and move on, one way or another. "I saw Dean Reynolds," he began. "He's in Maryland."

"I know," she said. "I saw him, too. But I wish I hadn't."

Haden softened his voice. "Why?"

"He's always reminded me of my dad," she said, "but now... Now there's nothing left but greed."

"It wasn't always that way."

She looked across the park and he followed her

gaze. A crowd of children, dressed in school uniforms, were having their pictures taken in front of the White House.

"I trusted him," she said. "And I shouldn't have."

"How were you supposed to know he'd gone bad?"

"You knew," she said simply. "After the Libyan deal went down. I should have known then, too."

"He meant more to you than he did to me," Haden replied. "He saw your talent at the Agency and made you into something special." He paused. "I saw your abilities and fell in love."

Her eyes went dark but before she could shutter her expression, Haden lifted her chin. Turning her face to his, he leaned closer. "And I still do," he whispered. "I love you, Meredith. I always have and I always will. There's only one problem."

Her eyelashes lowered and she started to draw away. "I know, Haden—"

"No, you don't."

Her gaze flew to his.

"You don't know what the problem is," he repeated, "and neither did I. If we'd both understood it better, we wouldn't be in the position we're in."

"What are you saying?"

"I shouldn't have pressed you like I did, but you could have told me the truth. If we'd each trusted one another more, things would have worked out a lot better for both of us."

She did pull away this time, her back going rigid. "I don't know what you're talking about—"

"I know about everything," he said softly. "Reynolds told me."

She stared at him in silence, her lips slightly parted. He couldn't think of anything else to do but put his arms around her and kiss her so he did. She resisted slightly, then the last of her hesitation dissolved. She pressed her body against his own, her mouth parting beneath his tongue. A second later, though, she stiffened and tilted backward to stare at him.

"Is this some kind of trick?"

He closed his eyes for a second then opened them. "I'm telling you the truth, Meredith. I had figured out most of it already, but I had no idea the president was involved. Reynolds told me."

"I didn't have a choice," she said. "I had to keep it secret."

"I know. And I understand. In fact, I love you all the more because of it. You did the right thing, Meredith. For yourself and for your county. I admire the guts it took. I should have accepted that you knew what you were doing."

"You're...okay with it?"

"Of course I am."

"But...?"

"But if we're taking this any further, the truth

will be what gets us there. Lies only lead to more lies and we already know where that takes us. We've been there. I don't want to go back and I know you don't want to, either."

Her hands tightened around his neck. "So how do we go forward? No one can ever know what I do. I can't discuss it with you. I have to keep my secrets. Can you live with the cloud that comes with that?"

"I'm going to have to," he said quietly. "Just like you're going to have to live with me being back at Langley."

Her mouth fell open. "You're leaving the field?"

"I just came from my White House briefing. The president asked me if I'd take Reynolds's place. I'll handle everything, except the running of the Operatives. You'd be moved to another department entirely. I said yes. Pending one point…"

"Pending one point…? What is that?"

"Before I decided for sure, I want to know how you feel about it. Nothing matters to me as much as that right now. I've lost you once. I don't intend for that to ever happen again. If taking that position would put our relationship in jeopardy, then I'm out of there and not looking back."

Her eyes filled unexpectedly. "Oh, Haden… I don't know what to say."

"Tell me you love me," he answered. "I think that would cover everything."

"I do love you!" she cried softly. "More than anything else in the world."

"Then we can work out the rest," he said with a grin, pulling her against him. "As long as we've got each other."

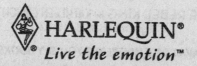

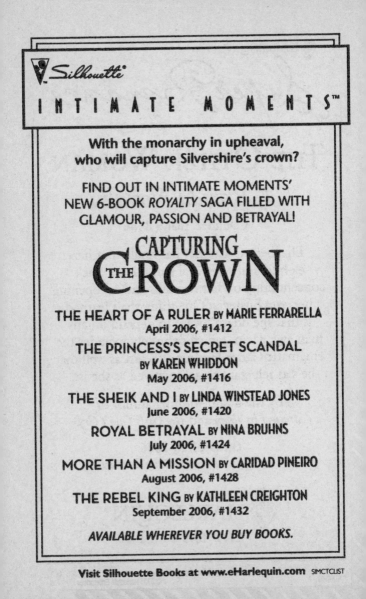

She had no choice but to grow up fast.

A woman reflects on her coming-of-age in this dramatic tale of a daughter torn between the love of her life and the family that needs her.

The Unspoken Years

by

Lynne Hugo

There comes a time in every woman's life when she needs more.

Sometimes finding what you want means leaving everything you love. Big-hearted, warm and funny, Flying Lessons is a story of love and courage as Beth Holt Martin sets out to change her life and her marriage, for better or for worse.

Flying Lessons

by

Peggy Webb

Available May 2006
TheNextNovel.com

HN42

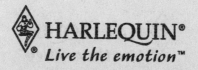

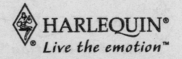